THE PATH OF RAINWATER

The Path of Rainwater

A novel

by

LAWRENCE WEILL

Adelaide Books
New York / Lisbon
2019

THE PATH OF RAINWATER
A novel
By Lawrence Weill

Copyright © by Lawrence Weill
Cover design © 2019 Adelaide Books

Published by Adelaide Books, New York / Lisbon
adelaidebooks.org
Editor-in-Chief
Stevan V. Nikolic

For any information, please address Adelaide Books
at info@adelaidebooks.org
or write to:
Adelaide Books
244 Fifth Ave. Suite D27
New York, NY, 10001

ISBN-10: 1-950437-02-7
ISBN-13: 978-1-950437-02-3

Printed in the United States of America

For Jennie

Contents

Foreword

Folks call me Rainwater. My name is James Rainwater but it got shortened somewhere along the line and now it's just Rainwater. It seems to suit me. I never really know what direction I'm going to go but I tend to take the easiest path I can find. It's the story of my life that I have chosen. I've been running downhill for a long time, taking the path of least resistance. It's the safest bet, I guess. I don't try to have a plan. I just go. If I don't know where I'm going, no one else will know either and that way, they don't know where to find me.

You meet a lot of folks on the road, some good, some bad, but mostly good. I've also met a lot of folks like me, moving, traveling, wandering.

I met this one fellow on the road. Called himself "Lightning" because he never landed the same place twice. That was his rule for traveling. I can understand that but that takes more planning and worrying about things than I want to do. Me, I've ended up in the same city before, even travelled down roads that were familiar. There have been lots of times I felt like settling in some place, but like the rain, I end up heading on down the road somewhere. Funny thing about that Lightning fellow, I saw him several times in my travels, never in the same place, like he said, but he was about as slow moving a guy as I ever met.

Green Pine Motor Lodge

I've heard people say, you don't know what you've got until it's gone. I guess sometimes that's true. But to me, it's also true you don't know what is gone until you got it. I mean, just about everything in the world is a trade-off of some sort. To get one thing you have to give up another. We think we know what we want, but most of the time, we have what we want the most and just don't know it. But funny things motivate people. I think lots of times, people decide to do something, or not to do it, because they're afraid they'll regret it later. Fear of regret is a poor motivator, if you ask me.

Rainwater watched the truck loaded with crates of chicken pass by him in a cloud of gravel dust and feathers. The squatty boxes were stacked high on the trailer. As the truck huffed by, spewing diesel fumes, a chicken fell from one of the crates somewhere along the edge of the truck and landed on the pavement. Rainwater walked towards the bird, watching as it flailed about a little, then sat still on the edge of the highway. It didn't move when Rainwater came nearer and he knew it was injured. He decided she would be a delicacy for him, fresh chicken, since she was destined to perish anyway. He reached down and picked up the hen by the neck. She squawked a couple of times before Rainwater twisted her neck, both to prepare her to be cleaned and to end her suffering. He reached into his pack and pulled out a plastic shopping bag he had found along some shunpike and put the bird in the bag and the bag back into his pack. He figured he had a few minutes to find a place to build a campfire and then clean and cook his found dinner.

Over the next hill and around a turn in the highway, Rainwater approached a crossroads. He saw it when he topped the hill, but it was still some distance away. The banks of the road were red clay, and up either side of the road were tall pine trees to the tops of the low hills. The crossroads was obvious precisely because it was the only area where the trees were cleared away, with maybe a combined store and gas station on one side, and, he saw as he came down the hill towards the turn, some kind of roadside stand. Rainwater headed for the intersection. It was not a special destination, of course, just the next one. When he got closer, a cola sign told him the store was called Taffy Corner Market. There were two gas pumps and a clapboard storefront with a couple of large windows and a front screen door with a Colonial Bread advertisement on the crossbar. The stand across the road had a single pickup truck backed up behind it where a man sat on the lowered tailgate. A wooden sign said it was the Taffy Fruit and Vegetable Stand. Evidently, Rainwater decided, he was in someplace called Taffy, Alabama. The warm weather had tired Rainwater, and he also worried about the freshness of chicken he had found. Around the edge of the little store was a fifty-five-gallon trash barrel that Rainwater briefly considered as a place to put the refuse from cleaning the bird, but he quickly discarded that notion. The barrel would reek in no time and he did not want to leave that for someone else. Still, the trash can had drawn him to the edge of the store property and that's when he saw the little motel behind it. Tucked into the tall trees was the Green Pine Cabins and Motor Lodge. It consisted of a half dozen small cabins gathered around a neatly mowed sward. On the near side of the cabins was another area, with no grass due to the pine needles, but with a picnic table, a heavy grill on a pedestal, a seesaw, and a swing set. Rainwater headed for the grill. He picked up pieces of pine as he walked. In the space between the store and the motel were several downed limbs. This would do nicely. If he could get the chicken cleaned and cooked before someone chased him off, it would be a great day. But first he had to clean it, which he knew was going to be messy.

Rainwater dragged some wood over to the grill. He was tempted to start the fire already so it would be going when he had the chicken cleaned, but he didn't want to leave the fire unattended, and there was always the possibility he might be chased off before that even happened. Besides, with no way to boil the feathers first, plucking might take longer than a fire would last unattended. He took the plastic bag with the dead chicken out and left his pack by the picnic table. He took his knife and the chicken and walked to the area between the motel and the store, then worked his way into the pines a bit.

He scraped away the neck feathers of the bird, then cut off the head with as clean a stroke as he could. He tied the feet together with a length of twine from his pocket and hung the bird on a stob of a pine and let the blood drain from the carcass onto a pile of pine straw he had raked together beneath it. While the blood was draining, he used a large stick to dig out a hole to put the entrails into once he was finished.

"Why'd you kill that chicken?"

Rainwater spun around to face the young voice that had startled him. Standing some ten yards from Rainwater was a boy, maybe twelve, in cut off shorts and a faded striped tee shirt. He had jet black hair that hung to his eyebrows. Rainwater nodded in greeting towards the boy. "Well, she was dead pretty much when I found her."

"You steal it?" The boy eyed him warily.

"No. No. It fell off on of those big chicken farm trucks. It fell off and I found it and now I'm going to cook it and eat it." Rainwater turned back around and started plucking the feathers from the bird and shoving them into the plastic bag.

"I bet you stole that chicken." The boy came up closer behind him but still kept his distance.

"Nope. Found it." Rainwater tugged at the feathers. It was slow going.

"My friend Marcus, he gave me a comic book and my Daddy said I stole it and he whupped me with a belt." The boy circled towards Rainwater's right, eyeing the processing of the hen closely. "I told him Marcus give it to me but he didn't believe me. Whupped me twice as hard cause he said I was lying."

"Sorry you got a whipping." Rainwater was getting some rythym going in the plucking and it was progressing. The bag was filling with feathers. Rainwater worried the father was going to come out from wherever the boy had come and cause trouble for Rainwater. Rainwater had been in plenty of fights before but he always tried to avoid them. He generally only fought when he was cornered or someone was taking something that was his that he valued. He didn't have much of anything but what he had was his and he hated when someone stole his stuff. He recalled now as he yanked off feathers that he had left his pack unattended by the grill. "Listen, I have to get this bird cleaned, okay? I'm afraid I don't have a lot of time to visit."

"That's okay." The boy had moved closer as he watched Rainwater and now he was standing right next to him. "How you gonna cook it? My momma, she likes to fry chicken. She's real good at it too. We ain't had no fried chicken in a while though." Rainwater stuffed the last of the feathers into the bag. There were still some small feathers, but he figured the fire would singe the rest off.

"Well, I'm going to roast this chicken over an open campfire, cowboy style." Rainwater wiped his knife on his thready khaki pants leg. The boy looked at Rainwater with wide eyes.

"Are you a cowboy?"

"Ha. No. I've done lots of jobs in my life, but I have never been a cowboy. I don't do horses, I'm afraid. But that doesn't mean I can't cook like a cowboy when I need to." Rainwater sized up the chicken then spread his feet apart. "Better stand back, boy. This gets pretty messy here."

"My name's Eddie." The boy lowered his eyes and stepped back.

"Eddie, you'd better stand back over here farther." Rainwater waved with his free hand. The boy moved where Rainwater had motioned.

"Yes, sir." He nodded, but his gaze was fixed on the chicken Rainwater was preparing to gut. Rainwater gave a glance at the boy. He hadn't been called "sir" in a long time.

"Thanks, Eddie."

"What's your name?"

"Folks call me Rainwater." He wiped the blade a couple of times on his pants leg as he sized up the cut.

"That's a funny name." Eddie stared now at the knife.

"Yeah, I guess it is. It used to be my last name, you know, like my father, but now it's pretty much my only name."

"I'm not supposed to tell you my last name." Rainwater raised his eyebrows and glanced over at the boy. When he did, the boy looked at the ground again.

"Don't recall asking."

"You live around here?" The boy maintained his gaze at the ground.

"Well, I'm from sort of all over, I guess. You?"

"I can't say." Eddie looked down still. Then Rainwater slit the bird open and raked out the entrails. They landed with a splash in the pile of pine straw below. Eddie jumped backwards. "Ew! That's so gross."

"Yeah, it is." Rainwater reached in several times to ensure the cavity was empty. He looked at his hand covered in the fluids from the hen. He hadn't really thought about how he would clean up afterwards. He slung what he could off his hand towards the pile of offal. "Yeah, it really is."

"There's a hose up by the cabin. It's where me and my sister Gina get drinks when we're staying in the playground while momma works."

Rainwater turned and looked at the boy. "Now that's some good news." He flipped his hands to sling off the fluid but he could feel the blood already drying on his hands, tightening the skin. He pushed the guts and bloody pine straw into the hole and then pushed the dirt over it, tamping the top by standing on the soft soil. "So, you and Gina like chicken?"

Rainwater picked up the hen and started for the playground. The boy followed behind, watching.

"Yes, sir. Gina, she likes the wings but I like the drumstick."

"Well, of course you do. That's the best part of a chicken, isn't it?" Rainwater found the hose behind a cabin. He washed the chicken as much as he could then scrubbed on his hands with the cool water and a bit of gravel from the drain area. Eddie tagged along beside him wherever Rainwater went. Back at the grill, Rainwater piled twigs in the fire box and struck a match to the bottom. The small pieces of pine caught quickly and he piled larger chunks on top. When the larger limbs began to flame, he put the grill bars down and lay the bird on top. The pin feathers sizzled as the fire licked around the skin of Rainwater's hen. He flipped it over. "Now, we just let her cook some." Rainwater shove a couple more medium sized branches into the fire. "The secret is to keep the fire going without getting it too hot." He stooped to peer into the little fire then stepped backwards to sit at the picnic table behind him, his back leaning against the table top. His mouth watered. Eddie stood next to him, also staring into the fire. "Nice little playground, isn't it?" Rainwater glanced around him. "It's good to have a place to play."

"Gina likes it. I guess it's okay. But playing is for kids. Mostly, I just keep an eye on Gina while Momma cleans."

"You're gonna be in trouble." The youthful voice behind him startled Rainwater out of his reverie. He began thinking of his defense against whatever trouble he was in for when he saw that it was a little girl and that she was not speaking to him but to Eddie. Eddie turned to face her.

"No, I'm not."

"Yes you are. Momma said not to talk to nobody while she was cleaning cabins."

Eddie's eyes widened. "Shush up, Gina!" Then he pointed at Rainwater. "This guy, he's a cowboy and he's cooking a cowboy chicken."

"Well, now, I'm not really a ..."

"Chickens can't be cowboys. They can't even ride a horse."

Rainwater guffawed. "Now, isn't that a picture in your head, a chicken trying to ride on a horse!" He leaned back and laughed and Eddie started laughing as well, then Gina.

Eddie slowed to a giggle. "I'd like to see a chicken trying to rope a cow." And the three dissolved into laughter again.

"What's going on here?" This voice was older. Rainwater turned his head and a dark-haired woman stood at the end of the picnic table, wiping her hands with a paper towel.

"Momma, that man is a cowboy and he's cooking his cowboy chicken." Gina pointed at Rainwater, who snorted another giggle.

"Now, I never said I was a cowboy, and chickens can't . . ."

"Lasso cows!" Eddie yelled and the three of them giggled some more.

The woman suppressed a smile and stepped closer. "You two go over to five and get cleaned up. I got some sandwiches made." She waved at the kids.

"But momma, I want . . ."

"Eddie, you take Gina over and you two wash your hands, like I said."

"But . . ."

"No 'buts'. Go on." The two children moped away.

Rainwater watched them amble familiarly across the playground towards a cabin. "I have plenty. I'd be happy to share."

"They'll be fine." The woman eyed the chicken cooking and swallowed. "I gotta say, it's been a while since them two laughed like that. It was good to hear. Thank you for that."

"It wasn't me. That little Gina is a smart little thing."

The woman looked up at him sharply. "Gina? You know my daughter's name? Who are you. He send you?"

Rainwater raised his hands before him and stood. "Your son told me her name. Nobody sends me anywhere. I didn't mean anything." The woman relaxed some. "People call me Rainwater. I'm just passing through with a dead chicken I found from a chicken truck." The woman looked over at the roasting bird and swallowed again. "There really is plenty, and I don't have a refrigerator for any left overs. If you and your children are free, I'd be honored if you'd join me for lunch."

"Why?"

"'Why?'"

"Why you want us to have lunch with you?" She kept her eyes focused on the roasting hen. It was starting to brown now, Rainwater saw, so he used two sticks chopstick style to turn it over. Juices ran out and onto the flame, sending a short flare up, and the scent of roasting chicken.

"Ma'am, I'm a drifter. I have pretty much nothing. Most of the time when I eat, it's through the kindness of others." He placed the rough chopsticks on the picnic table and turned to face the woman now. "I'm just paying it forward a little, that's all. If a man lives off of kindness, he should sow a lot of seeds." She cocked her head to one side and looked at him now for the first time in a while. It was as if she had been mesmerized by the cooking bird.

"I ain't allowed to cook in the cabins. I haven't had a hot meal in God knows."

Rainwater shrugged. "So, you'll join me?"

"Let me grab them kids." She backed away a couple of steps, then turned and marched away.

Rainwater looked at the chicken. It still had a little ways to go. But as a dinner for five, it looked meager. Then he remembered the vegetable stand. He shoved a couple of larger pieces of wood onto the edge of the fire, then trotted over to the stand. The old man sitting on the tailgate of the pickup didn't rise at first. Rainwater mentally counted his coins in pocket. "How much for fives ears of corn?"

"Buck fifty."

"I'll do it." Rainwater reached into his pocket and fished out the quarters and dimes and nickels, many of which he found along the road. The man stood up slowly, deliberately, and tossed the corn into a plastic shopping bag labelled Piggly Wiggly with a cartoon of a pig's head on it. Rainwater handed him his coins.

"You want some apples?" He motioned to a stack of dark red apples. "They're local." One apple was cut in half and perched on top for shoppers to see the bright white fruit, but the edges were turning just a tad brown.

"They all look like that?" Rainwater nodded towards the apple that was turning. The man shot him a look.

"Nope. Just been sitting there for a bit." The vendor reached for the apple.

"I'll give you a nickel for that one." The man raised his eyebrows at Rainwater. "Got two hungry kids who won't mind the edges, I'm sure."

The old man tossed the apple into the bag with the corn. "You can have it, no charge."

"Thank you, sir." Rainwater grabbed the sack and trotted back across the road to the play area. The fire was lower but still going enough to catch the additional limbs Rainwater now added. He lined the ears of unshucked corn along the edge of the grill and poked the coals with a heavy stick to even out the heat. The woman was coming across the parking area now, one child on each side running to keep up with their mother. She carried a several items in her cupped hands in front of her as she marched across the parking lot, past the seesaw and over to the picnic table where Rainwater sat.

She poured out the items in her hands onto the table while the two children watched from either side of her. "I got a bunch of salt and pepper I saved from restaurants while we was moving around. Figured they'd come in handy." She handed him a sandwich bag of full of packets. "Got some plastic forks too." She looked over towards the chicken. "What? You got corn too? That sure was some truck you followed, mister."

Rainwater gave a chuckle. "Just 'Rainwater.' I got them over at the stand for next to nothing."

"We're having corn on the cob and cowboy chicken!" Gina yelled. The woman looked around her nervously.

"Hush up now, Gina. You and Eddie go play on the swings til the foods ready, okay?"

"I don't wanna . . ." Eddie whined.

"Go play." She barked sharply.

"Yes'm." Eddie lowered his head and took his sister's hand. "C'mon, Gina." He slunk away. Gina ran in front of him as they neared the swing set, jumped onto a metal swing and started kicking her legs back and forth to gain momentum.

"Push me, Eddie. Push me." She kept swinging her legs out but she was not getting any movement. Eddie came around behind her and pushed her. "Higher." Gina kept kicking her feet out. "Higher."

"That high enough, Gina. It ain't safe to go any higher." Eddie stood behind her, his arms hanging straight at his sides, watching her.

Rainwater realized neither he nor the woman had spoken for a few moments. He turned his head to look at her, but she was still staring at her children. As if sensing his returned focus, she looked back at Rainwater now "He's real good with her. I don't know what I'd do if it weren't for him." She finished emptying her hands onto the table. There was a small stack of clear plastic cups, several different sized napkins folded in varying shapes, some in plastic bags with forks included. She stood the plastic cups up. "These are used, but I washed them, so they're clean. They come from the cabins. Each day I gather up the cups and wash them and if they don't have scratches or anything on them, I cover them with plastic wrap and use a hairdryer to made them look like they're all sanitized and everything." Rainwater gave her a puzzled look. "Oh, the owners, they told me to do that. I didn't come up with that one myself." She arranged the items in short rows along the edge of the table. "So these are clean, just weren't good enough to reuse." Rainwater processed what he was being told.

"So, the cups in the room . . ."

"He takes good care of his sister, but he just isn't the same these days." She looked over at her children. Eddie still stood behind Gina, occasionally pushing her, but mostly just standing there, stone faced. "He won't play."

"Well, ma'am, he does seem . . ."

"'Ma'am'? Oh my, no one's 'ma'am'-ed me in a long time. My name's Leslie. Or Momma," She nodded towards the children. Rainwater followed her eyes to the swing set. He stood now and turned the corn and poked at the coals beneath them again. The corn was coming along.

"Corn's nearly done, Leslie. And this bird is cooked." Rainwater took his knife and cut the chicken in half. The juices ran out and flared the fire. He cut as many pieces as he could, figuring kids might eat smaller portions. He didn't want to waste any of the meat.

"Eddie! Gina! Come on!" The children ran over excitedly. Leslie handed them a small bar of soap. "Go wash your hands over at the hose, then come on back for Mr. Rainwater's cowboy chicken. Here, Eddie, fill these up with water too." She handed the boy a stack of plastic cups.

Rainwater smiled. So now it was his recipe. "It's just 'Rainwater.' No one calls me mister anything these days." Eddie and Gina raced to the hose and washed their hands. Leslie took napkins and spread them out on the table. Rainwater shucked the corn, shoving the husks into the Piggly Wiggly bag. The pieces of roasted chicken next to the deep yellow and brown of the roasted corn looked good. Rainwater's mouth watered. The children returned and hopped onto the bench of the picnic table and started tearing at the chicken pieces before them.

"Wait. Eddie, Gina, you mind your manners now." The children stopped and looked up at their mother. "Eddie, will you say the blessing?"

"Yes'm." He lowered his eyes and folded his hands before him. Gina copied his movements, as did Rainwater. "God is great. God is good. Let us thank Him for our food. Amen." He looked up. "Now?"

Leslie smiled. "Yes, you can go ahead and eat now." She took out some packets of salt and pepper and seasoned her corn and the chicken breast before her. She passed the plastic bag over to Rainwater. All four fell silent. Rainwater watched the two children eating ravenously and smiled as he ate. It felt good to make them so happy. Both children ate seconds on the chicken and when they were done, the bird was gone.

"Momma, can we go play now?" Gina wiped her hands on her shirt.

"Wait. Don't use your shirt. Girl." Leslie shook her head as she reached across the table to wipe her daughter's hands which were mostly clean now. "Here, you two go wash up, then go play." She handed the soap to Eddie again and the two trotted over to the hose. Leslie gathered the bones and corn cobs and carried them over to a trash barrel. Eddie and Gina returned with the soap and lay it next to the stack of plastic cups. Leslie came back and gathered together the few napkins and seasoning packets left and put it all together with the cups and the soap.

"I've got dessert too." Rainwater reached into his pack and retrieved the halved apple he had set aside. "Here you go." He handed each child a half. They looked up at Leslie. She nodded and they retreated to the seesaw to eat their treat.

"That's mighty nice of you, sir. That's maybe the best meal they've had in a while."

"My pleasure."

"They let me stay in cabins that aren't rented in return for cleaning, but I'm not supposed to cook nothing on account of the smells and such. Lord knows, the guests leave lots of smells you don't even want to talk about, but they're paying customers so that makes it different, I guess." She watched her children eating apples.

"Huh. I suppose that's not a bad arrangement. They pay you too?"

"No, I clean and they let us stay. It works out. There have only been a couple of times the place was full, so we've made do. When they were full, I just pretended with the kids we were camping in our car, but Eddie knows what the deal is. But he plays along for Gina's sake."

"They don't pay you?" Rainwater glanced over.

"No. But that's okay."

Rainwater shook his head. "How do you live? What about food and everything?"

"Well, you know sometimes folks leave tips for the cleaning and I get to keep that. And we've got a place to stay. I wash our clothes with the towels. People never use all the soap and shampoo, so we got that. It works." She shrugged.

"Seems like they maybe could pay you something though." Rainwater raised an eyebrow.

"No, I don't want them to." Leslie looked down at her hands.

"What? Why?"

"If they pay me, they gotta get my last name and put down my social security somewhere. I don't need that. No, I don't need that." She cut a glance over at Rainwater and shook her head.

"Oh." Rainwater nodded. "You know, there are resources . . ."

"I know all about resources, thank you. He's got more resources than I do, so maybe it's best I fly low to the ground." She gave Rainwater an even look. He nodded.

"I understand. I do understand about the resources others have."

Eddie and Gina came back now with tiny apple cores in their hands. "Momma, what do we do with the core?" Gina held her hand up.

"Just throw them in the trash, honey."

"Wait." Rainwater swung his legs back over the bench of the table. "Bring them over here." He carried his fire poking stick over to the edge of the play area. The pine needles were sparser and tufts of grass stood up from the red clay. The two children followed him. He dug two round holes into the dirt about ten feet apart. "Put them in here." Each child dropped their gnawed core into a hole. Rainwater walked over and mashed the holes closed with his foot. "Okay, now every day, you water these and one day there will be two apple trees right here, and you can eat apples whenever you want."

"Really?" Gina looked up with amazement.

"Really?" Eddie's face was more curiosity.

"Really. Now go get a couple of cups of water and get them started." The two children ran back to the table, retrieved plastic cups, and then headed for the hose. Rainwater returned to the table and gathered his pack while he watched them dart over, sloshing most of the water as they went, and pour the remainder on the indentations in the ground. They scurried back and forth, carrying, sloshing, and watering. "That's enough. Don't want to drown them," he called. He slung the pack over his shoulder.

"We won't be here that long, of course." Leslie watched her children return to the swing set. Gina climbed on one swing, Eddie on the other. Eddie kicked his legs to start the motion, leaning forward then back. The swing moved back and forth.

"Like this, Gina." He leaned and kicked and his sister imitated his motions.

"Yeah, but that doesn't matter, does it?" Rainwater turned and walked towards the crossroads.

"No, it doesn't." Leslie stood and called after him. "Thanks again, Rainwater." Rainwater raised his free hand in acknowledgement, walked through the small wooded area between the motel and the store, then turned the corner. Leslie watched the man at the vegetable stand tracing Rainwater's path with the turn of his head. She sat and watched her children playing on the swings.

Kentucky Back Roads

You know, it's enough to make you shake your head when you think about it. I mean seems like people work all their lives and what've they go to show for it? A trailer in Florida and kids who'll stick you in the nursing home when you get to be a nuisance. Pity, I tell you. Now you take a man who works in his shop, maybe he fixes televisions or something. After a while, he knows all about them TV's. Why, he can just look at a TV and see that he's gotta put a new oscillator or something in. 'Fore long, people call him Jones, the TV man. He's walkin' down the street and people say "Hi Mr. Jones. Listen my picture ain't right..." and he tells 'em what to do and they're happy as larks. Now that Mr. Jones, the TV man, he means something to those people. He's more real to them than some fellow who don't do nothin'. Folks know about the things he knows and they like that. But Mr. Jones, he doesn't see it that way. He can't wait to sell his little store and buy a trailer and move to Florida. For what? Down there, he ain't a TV man, he's just another old man in a trailer. Seems like people can't wait to give up the very thing that makes them what they are.

A steady wind lashed September grasses and a cool sun faded the day pale. Birds braving chilling breezes chirped and chattered in scattered clumps of brush and trees along the road. A lone man bent into the damp afternoon, leaning down the road from the hilltop, passed the orchard with gnarled apple trees and twisted peach trees, passed yellow fields where giant rolls of hay stood like sentinels. He trudged to a gate that hung in a gap of a haphazard stone fence. The dog in the yard barked and two more ran barking around the peeling frame house. His grey overcoat hung loose about his stooping, gaunt shoulders. His fading tweed hat was limp. A grey beard stood out from his chin and cheeks. He stared at the dogs yapping in the yard, then walked to the little white house. The dogs did not bother him as he stepped across the holes in the porch to the screen door.

He knocked, and the loose door rattled. The dogs circled behind him. Now he pounded on the screen. Finally, he called, "Anyone home?" He peered around the edge of the house to where the dogs had run from and called again. "Hello?" The dogs wagged and barked beside him.

"Yeah, what can I do for you?" The voice from the doorway behind him made him jump. At first he thought it to be a man's, but as he spun, he saw a large woman with long hands and a short, round face glowering at him. "You want something?"

"Well yeah, I need some work. Low wages, just food, a few bucks, enough to keep me going." He stared at her light blue print dress, all faded and worn, her wrinkled squinting eyes and grey hair pulled into a bun atop her head. He smiled a practiced smile.

She returned a frown exaggerated on her coarse skin. She paused in the doorway, holding the screen ajar, staring down at the grey man. "Just what is it you do?"

"Odd jobs: carpentry, clean up, labor; pretty much what you want done. I can work hard as you please. Folks know me as Rainwater, ma'am. I'm willing to work."

She glanced down at Rainwater's hands. She looked at his rough knuckles and cracked skin. Pushing the door further she finally answered him, "Well I got too much to do to turn down cheap labor; come on in." She nodded in to the house and he stepped past her into the bleak living room.

The furnishings were bare, at best; a round overstuffed chair in a faded floral, a worn, tattered rug, two small ladder back chairs and a small table beside the open porch window. The pastel walls were bare except for the spider webs in the corners. A doorway opposite the front door led to the rest of the house.

He stepped into the center of the chairs and felt conspicuous in the empty room. The air blew brisk through the open window, so he kept his overcoat on. She followed him and filled the room with her presence, though now she spoke more softly.

"Well, Rainwater, you say? Where you coming from?"

"I was over down in Birmingham, but there's no use staying if you can't find work. The strike's got all the men off and you can't get a job with all of them out there looking too. I'm trying to get someplace new, maybe Louisville. There must be something there, as big as it is." He sat suddenly and familiarly, taking off his hat and holding it in his lap. He stared at his hat. "I don't know what's to happen when a person can't get work."

"Well, you want work? I've got plenty to do around here. You do a good job and you'll get paid. The food's plain but I'll make plenty. And if you need to, you can sleep in the shed tonight before you leave tomorrow." She stood stolid on the dilapidated rug.

29

"I'm at your service, Ma'am." Rainwater waved his hands and lifted his head. Long white curls dangled about his ears.

"Well, okay then," she replied, "let's get to work. Better take off that coat so you can move better. I got plenty to do; fences need mending, the barn needs some boards on it. The front porch is falling apart, but I guess you saw that already. There's lots more, too." She was walking out toward the kitchen and he stood and followed her. She walked through the kitchen and headed for the back door, preparing a mental list of tasks for Rainwater to perform. He stepped behind her and called her.

"Ma'am, excuse me, but I'm already pretty hungry." He paused in anticipation. She turned and looked at him, reached to a bowl on the table and tossed him a small green and red apple. He caught it, looked at it for a moment and then ate it hurriedly as he stepped behind his benefactress into the yard.

She took long strides through the small yard and chickens scurried to make way for her. Her long dress nipped about her ankles, revealing heavy black shoes. The small fence around the yard was falling down in at least three places and the white paint was visible only slightly. Hens hopped through the broken slats and scratched the grass outside the yard. Beyond the gate that hung limply at an opening on the fence, where the broad-shouldered woman now stood, an old barbed wire fence traipsed up a hillside. A barn with loose grey boards and large doors held closed with wooden bolts stood beyond the yard just to the right, and a muddy, rutted path led past it to the hill crest.

But the woman was not to the barn yet; she stared at the fence and the drooping roof of the back porch. "You can start with the fence here," she waved. "Got some wood up by the barn: had it for some time and never got around to using it.

I think there's some white paint in the barn, too, but I don't know if it's any good any more. Tools are inside the house. I got some big four by fours for the porch; all you got to do is push them under the roof and use the sledge to straighten it up, least that's what my neighbor suggested." She waved toward the porch. "Them steps is getting pretty rotten, too; better put some new ones on. I got some sawhorses around here somewhere, but I ain't used them for a long time, so you'll just have to look around until you find them. There's no telling where they might be. There's plenty of paint out in the shed on the other side of the barn, and nails should be there, too. Anything else you need, just ask and I'll see if I can find it." She paused, her hands on her hips. "You start on that and I'll see what needs to be done up at the barn." She marched to the barn, her energy up from the prospect of chores getting done. Rainwater followed behind to get the wood and nails for his work, but she was inside the barn before he reached the road.

He stooped over the greying wood, stacked haphazardly beside the barn. The wood had been there for several years and some had rotted. A brown snake slithered from the far end of the pile through the blackberry bushes that led back to the row of trees on the hill. He threw his apple core at the rustling grasses where the snake crawled. Wiping his hands on his baggy khaki pants, he loaded some spikes in his arms and carried them to the gate, and dropped them in the dust beside the fence. The chickens cackled beside around him and watched him work.

He straightened and felt the catch in his back. He grimaced as he dug his knuckles into the small of his back. He turned to go to the barn and arched his back.

In the shed, it was dark, and Rainwater squinted in the dusty light that shone through the cracks between the boards.

On a long table were several reed baskets filled with various nuts, screws, bolts, nails, and washers. Rainwater picked through one basket but found no nails small enough. He reached to a pile of cardboard boxes and found some brads in one. He found a brush and some white paint and caught the last glint on two rusty steel hinges as he walked out of the shed.

Outside, the sun was at its brightest, though the cool made it seem drab. He turned the corner around the barn and saw the woman waving her arms in wide circles about the yard with the hens scurrying around her. As he walked across the road with his armload of supplies, she turned and watched him. Walking to the gate, Rainwater smiled and she turned to feed the chickens closer to the house. As he sorted through the tools she had brought out of the house for a hammer, she spoke loudly across the yard to him.

"I also got a window in the bathroom needs fixing. Got the glass for it last month, but I ain't had the time to get it in. Had a piece of plywood in there since I broke it. Well, I didn't really break it; the wind did. That is, the wind made the window slam and it broke. I got the pane in the kitchen." She paused, watching the hens scramble. "I thought I'd make some stew tonight. It ain't real fancy but folks around here used to say it was the best you would eat. Of course, I don't cook that much nowadays." She shook out her apron now and the chickens bickered for the last kernels. Rainwater pounded on the gate he had taken off the fence. She walked into the house and Rainwater looked after her for a moment. He looked back at the gate he was kneeling on; grey pine slats nailed in a simple row; fading wood against the pale brown dust of the earth below it. The hammer beat on the nail head and the boards stiffened. He held the repaired unit in his cold hands and measured the hinges against the heavy gate post. He tapped the nails into the holes, holding the gate with his knees. The top hinge tight, he squared the gate and placed the second. The gate hung low on the latch side and tended to close, but he decided it was good because the chickens would be less likely to run out it the gate closed. Of course, until he fixed the fence, it would make little difference. He sat beside the pile of wood and lit a cigarette, cupping his match against the chilly wind and hunching his shoulders to ward off his shivers. He looked at the gate approvingly and then at the paint; yes, now he must paint it to make it look right. It would be as good as new then.

The woman walked back and forth in the kitchen and Rainwater saw her pass the window from the counter to the stove and back. Occasionally, he saw the refrigerator door open in the window of the back door. The light gave a warm glow above the table, turning everything slightly yellow. The day began to wane and the breeze had blown heavy clouds up from the horizon. The woman's great arms moved methodically above the counter. Now she reached to the cupboard above her and now she bent to the cabinet at her knees. The dogs slept under the back porch. The chickens had scattered after their meal. Steam began to rise from the stove and the windows began to fog, making the kitchen seem even warmer and more inviting. Rainwater drew the smoke from his cigarette heavily, the orange glow of fire racing toward his mouth. He placed the spent butt in the dirt beside him and covered it with dust.

Rising from his seat, Rainwater pushed his knuckles into the small of his arched back. He shook the can of paint in his coarse hands, placed it next to the gate, and, after popping the lid off with a screwdriver, dipped the dark, smooth bristles of the brush into the velvety white liquid. The paint dripped in a steady, oily stream back into the can and Rainwater brushed the excess against the side of the opening. The dry wood absorbed the oil immediately; it would probably take two coats. He covered both sides of the once grey wood and dabbed into the corners where the stays were nailed. The white paint dribbled into the brown dust in tiny patterns and great drops as Rainwater rushed to finish. He stood away from the gate, brush in hand and looked for bare spots. After a few last minute touches, he replaced the lid on the paint can and tapped it closed. He placed the brush on top of the can and stood up straight. It looked good; the woman would have to buy a new gate to do as well. Rainwater smiled. He looked toward the kitchen, glowing warmly golden against the increasingly grey sky, but the woman was not in sight. The pot still steamed on the stove and Rainwater's mouth watered to think of it. He was hungry, but he had not yet finished his work.

The fence would be next; after all, she had mentioned it first. Rainwater walked around the fence to inspect it. Several posts had rotted away at their bases. Six slats were out here, three there and four, no, five in the corner. He picked over the wood with his hands stiffening in the growing cold and rising wind. He had to work quickly or it would get too dark to work. The day was fading rapidly. He drove long boards into the ground on either side of the posts and secured them together with long nails. He trimmed smaller boards for the slats and slipped them into the wire framework, pinching the metal with pliers to hold the boards. The air had grown moist and Rainwater could see his breath steaming as he worked on the fence. By the time he finished, the sky was a heavy grey black. A light mist began falling and Rainwater packed the tools to take them into the house. As he latched the tool box closed, the woman pushed the screen open at the back door and stepped onto the drab boards of the porch.

"Come on in, Rainwater," she called, waving her long hands. "It's too dark to do anymore tonight. Supper's all ready. Come on in out of the rain."

He walked to the porch with the tool box in one hand. She was holding the door for him and the light behind her made her softer. He smiled and she lowered her head as he stepped past her. On the table the stew, brown and thick, steamed in a large old bowl. Another bowl with a chip in one side held a mountain of mashed potatoes. He put the tools in a corner and turned to the woman.

"I'd like to clean up a bit, Ma'am."

"Sure. The washroom's right through that doorway to your right. You go right ahead and I'll get the beans on the table." She turned and reached to the cabinet as he peered into the darkened hallway. "The light's right next to the door," she called without looking. A familiar click told her he had found it. She heard the sink water running as she placed the last bowls on the table. She stood back and checked to see if all was in order, wiping her hands on her apron. The dishes were faded and had a few cracks, and the mismatched dinnerware seemed awkward on the stained linen napkins, but she felt proud of the meal and beamed over it. She untied her apron and tossed it on the counter. As she poured deep black coffee, Rainwater returned and stood behind his chair while she replaced the pot and sat at her seat. His eyes panned the table as he sat.

"It certainly looks delicious, Ma'am," he said. "I can't remember when I ever ate so good. I'm very grateful, Ma'am."

"Save your compliments until you taste it; it might not be worth it." She smiled across the table at him. She looked at him slowly. "It's been a long time since a man sat at this table. It's been a long time since anyone besides myself sat here." She paused and looked at Rainwater's heavy beard. "Will you say grace?"

"Sure," he closed his eyes and lowered his head. "Heavenly Father, bless this food this good woman has worked so hard to fix. Amen." The woman looked up but said nothing. She passed him the bowls and watched as he filled his plate with food. His face was tired and grey and the artificial light deepened the lines on his brow. She served herself and began to eat. The room grew quiet. Rainwater ate hungrily and accepted unhesitatingly when she offered him second helpings. She beamed at his unspoken compliment. They spoke very little as they ate; he stared at his plate while she gazed slowly at the gentle, old man who had wandered to her table. When they had finished eating, she poured him another cup of coffee and he sat back in his chair.

"Like I said, Ma'am, I can't remember when I ate so good. Thank you." He patted his sides.

"Well, I'm glad you liked it. It ain't often I get a chance to entertain and I enjoyed it." She smiled at him and he returned it.

"So, you run this farm by yourself?" he asked.

"Yeah, more or less. You can see there's a lot of things that just don't get done, but I manage. All I got is the chickens, a little vegetable patch, and a couple of cows up on the hill, but everything's done paid for and I don't need much. I got some pension from my husband, rest his soul, and that pays the taxes and such. My kids tell me I should sell out and move to the city with them, but this is home to me. I belong here. Besides, nobody'd want this old farm. I couldn't get a plug nickel for this old place. Without me, I figure it'd be deserted. But I like staying here. Oh, it gets lonely sometimes; not too many people come out since my husband died. My two boys live in the city now, can't keep them home anymore." She paused, holding her coffee. "The kids all want to go to the university and live in the city," she spoke to herself as much as she did to

Rainwater, "but it's their lives. Mrs. Howard from up the road comes by sometimes and takes me to town to do my shopping once every couple of weeks, so I get out some. Mostly, I just stay around here and to my chores." She paused, slightly embarrassed at her confessions. She sipped her coffee. "But what about you, Rainwater? Where are your folks?"

He paused a moment then answered with a shrug. "There's not much to tell, really. I've got some kin in Ohio. I used to think about them sometimes when I passed through. But I guess I just don't pass that way much anymore. The road is home to me, I guess. I came through Birmingham to see a friend of mine from the merchant marines, but he wasn't around. I don't guess I really expected him to be there, it was just a reason to go somewhere. I went down there after coming through Evansville from up around Indianapolis. I had been in Minnesota before that, but it was getting too cold up north. I've been thinking about going back down to New Orleans for the winter, maybe do some crabbing. I don't know. I'm getting too old for the road. Sleeping outside in all kinds of weather, eating what you can when you can. And it's really hard when you get off the main highways because nobody will give you a ride. I sure can't walk too far anymore." He spoke and shook his head and the white curls dangled about his ears.

She listened and drank her coffee. Her brow scowled. "Ain't you ever had a home?"

"Oh, sure, once," he said, half smiling. "I got married as soon as I got out of the service to the prettiest girl in the whole town. That was up in Cincinnati," he waved. "We moved to Florida during the war and I went back into the merchant marines. While I was out to sea, she had twins, girls. Smartest, prettiest little things you ever saw. When I got back we went back up to Ohio and I tried to get work in some of the warehouses in Cincinnati but I hurt my back and couldn't keep a job. I tried all kind of ways to make ends meet. And then there was . . ." Rainwater gazed off to his right, as if remembering something, then returned his focus to the woman across from him. "Well, things got worse and worse and then the . . ." He paused, then shook his head, as if erasing something. "Well, one day I left and the missus took the girls and went back to her folks, I suppose. I guess I've been a couple of thousand places since then. But it's hard to find work anymore; no one wants to hire an old man with a bad back and no home." He felt himself grow melancholy and shook it off. "But I always get by. Something always seems to show up when I need it," he shrugged.

"Well, I ain't got much to pay you with, but if you're looking for a place to stay for a while, I got lots of work that needs to done. A lot of people need help with their tobacco fields around here, too." She stopped then abruptly. He nodded, partially out of gratitude, partially at her embarrassment, and the room fell silent. The wind whistled around the house and crickets and katydids called from the porch. The woman sat holding her coffee, staring down at the deep brown liquid, and thinking about this stranger so like herself, not so much despite their differing lifestyles, but because of them. They were both at home in their desolate lives; both independent, both lonely. Rain began to fall in heavy drops on the window above the sink. She replaced her cup in its cracked saucer and broke the quiet. "Well, I'd better get on these dishes if they're to get done. You want some more coffee?"

"Don't mind if I do, Ma'am." He pushed his cup across the table. She poured the steaming coffee and turned to stack the dishes on the counter top. He watched her move from the table to the sink and back. She hummed softly as the dishes clanked and the forks clanged creating a curious music. He sipped his coffee and replaced the cup in its saucer. Suds swelled in the steaming sink. Rainwater's back hurt. He watched her washing the dishes and rubbed his back with one hand. She was still humming, but so quietly that no one tune could be heard. "No, Ma'am, I don't guess I'm too suited for county life; I've always kind of liked the city myself. I need lots of people around. Maybe when I get to Louisville, I'll get some work and be able to stay a while and enjoy it some, maybe get a house. Yes, Ma'am, I sure would like to have a nice place like yours." He circled the room with his eyes. "You're lucky to have a nice home like this." He looked up to her broad shoulders bent over the sink.

"Your home is where you find it, ain't it?" She turned and looked at him. "And maybe that's a blessing, too."

"I guess maybe it is," he sighed. "But I don't know."

"Not many people have seen what you've seen, Rainwater."

"Not many would want to, Ma'am. Care if I smoke?" He shook his head, took a long drink of coffee, and lit a cigarette. "You know, it makes me sad sometimes when I visit someplace I've been before. Towns change, new highways come and take all the people to the cities, the old people die, and pretty soon it's all different. It's a pity. People don't seem to know who they are anymore; they just take what they can get." He took a long draw on his cigarette and she placed a clean saucer on the table for his ashes. "You just can't take things for granted."

"Why keep travelling, then? If it makes you sad, why not stop? Why not stay around here and work on the farm and help these folks around here. They're not fancy, just folks, but they're honest, good people, and they appreciate a good day's work." She sat opposite him and crossed her great arms on the table. He smiled and looked in her round face to where the wrinkles met at the corners of her eyes. He looked back at his coffee and the smoke that rose and circled from his cigarette like a thin, grey highway.

"No Ma'am, ain't found my home yet. Guess I'll have to keep travelling until I do. There's lots of places I've never been. Maybe one of them will hit me as home and I'll settle down. Who knows?" He paused, then looked up and forced a smile. "But I've got a friend in Louisville who can help me get work and I'll be fine. You know, he's always telling me to stop by and see him and now I think, by golly, I'll do it." He looked at her and snuffed the cigarette in the saucer.

She set her lips as she rose from the table. "Well, I must excuse myself. My morning comes early and I've got to get my rest. I'll get you some blankets and you can sleep on the floor in the kitchen tonight. It's too cold to sleep in the shed." She rummaged in the closet in the hallway. "If you're still here tomorrow, I got lots more work that needs to be done," she called as she pulled the bed covers from the shelf. She dropped the heavy blankets in the corner and walked back down the hallway. "There's ham and biscuits for breakfast." She went to her room and sat on the quilt on her for a moment. "Well, if that's what makes him happy, he's a right to it," she said aloud and she shook her head as she began to undress for bed.

The morning sun shone through the bedroom window and the woman bustled around the bedroom. She hummed quietly as she pulled the quilt under her pillow and rubbed her hand across the night stand beside her bed. She slipped quietly into the kitchen, but Rainwater was gone. The blankets were folded neatly on the floor where she had left them. She walked to the front porch, pulled open the heavy door, and looked at the gate that hung limply between the stone fences.

Beyond the road, the grass shone golden in the morning sun. The old woman pushed aside the screen and walked onto the porch, stepping across the holes. She stared down the road that led to the highway. The dogs crawled form beneath the house and barked beside the woman. She gazed at the hillsides in the distance then turned to the house.

A loud thump echoed from the back and the woman walked heavily through the house to investigate. A large four-by-four leaned against the outside wall and Rainwater pulled a sledge hammer across the yard. The woman smiled, opened the door, and called to him, "Breakfast won't be a minute." Rainwater looked up and waved with his free hand. The woman gathered her energy. She began hurrying about in the kitchen, clanging the pans quickly and rattling the dishes in haste. She had left the door open and Rainwater could see her through the screen. He smelled biscuits baking and heard the ham sizzling. Rainwater propped the post between the floor and the roof of the porch and raised the sledge. His back hurt from sleeping on the floor and he winced.

This woman could use some help, he thought, and he could use the shelter and food, what with winter coming on. She was broad and plain and not much to look at but she was kind and generous and what's more, she needed him. It was not a bad place, though it needed some repairs. It was a place with lots of memories, the harshness of life softened with time. He pounded the post, driving it under the roof which creaked as it rose. The morning warmed and Rainwater began to get wet with perspiration. He hit the broad board, splitting it some at the base, but straightening it. He put the hammer down and arched his back, driving his knuckles into his spine. The woman came to the door.

"Breakfast is on."

"Good. I'm starved!" He entered the door and went to wash. The old woman watched him pass and smiled. As they began to eat, she felt he belonged there, sitting stiffly at the table, hungrily eating biscuits and ham.

"Fine work you been doin', Mr. Rainwater."

"Just Rainwater. And thank you, Ma'am. I try to do my best." He pushed a piece of biscuit into his mouth.

"Could use lots more chores gettin' done, yes sir. That porch has been ready to drop for a year, I guess. Just can't find good work no more. And that fence. I can't remember when it looked so good. Yes sir, you've been doin' real good."

"Thank you, Ma'am." He sipped his coffee.

"Yeah, I got lots to do around here. Got that window. Front porch is real bad, too. I could have a milking cow if I had any fences."

Rainwater grabbed another biscuit.

"Lots of work around here needs doin'. Neighbors'll be putting up tobacco soon."

Rainwater did not answer, but he heard. The work was not bad, at least it was honest. And he might be able to get a cot somewhere to sleep on. The biscuits were sweet and the ham hearty and filling. And no one knew him around here.

"You ever work tobacco?" she was asking. "Hard work, but good pay."

Rainwater stabbed another piece of ham with his fork. "No Ma'am, never did." He placed another bite in his mouth.

She grew quiet, then lowered her voice. "Why don't you stay, Rainwater? Don't you ever want to stay and get to know people?"

Rainwater looked up at her and swallowed his half-chewed bite. "Yes, Ma'am, I do get the urge to settle sometimes. Truth is, I'm tempted to take you up on your kind offer right now, as a matter of fact." He smiled and his face flushed.

"Good!" she beamed, pushing from the table. "You'll like it around here, I'll bet." She rose in excitement. "We'll find you someplace to stay and . . ."

"No, Ma'am, I'm tempted but I can't. It's just not me. I can't do it."

She stopped, her disappointment obvious. "But you'd like to stay, wouldn't you?" She sat awkwardly.

"Yes'm." Rainwater rubbed his back. "But I guess I just need the road under my feet. I'd like to stay, but I wouldn't be happy. I need to see some more of the world, I guess. I thank you for the work and food and place to sleep, but it's time I moved on, Ma'am."

The woman stood up abruptly and poured another cup of coffee for herself and one for Rainwater. They sat silent for some time as Rainwater finished his cup. The woman looked at her cup, but did not drink.

"Well I thank you again, Ma'am. I got to be going." He stood and bowed slightly at the waist and his back tightened. He went over to the corner and picked up his coat and bag. The woman followed him with her eyes.

"Let me get you some money for your work." The woman started to leave but Rainwater raised his hand.

"No, Ma'am. You've paid me plenty." She turned and looked him.

"You ought to stay, Rainwater," she said finally. "There's nothing on that road." Her voice was heavy and slow. Rainwater was at the door now.

"Yes'm, I know that." He pushed open the screen and stepped across the porch. The woman followed him to the door and pushed it open.

"Is it me?" she finally asked. "I'm too pushy, aren't I? My kids are always telling me I'm too bossy."

Rainwater stopped and turned. He looked at her evenly. "No Ma'am, you're why I'd like to stay." He stepped closer to her and touched her shoulder. It was strong under the faded dress. He looked into her eyes and they were wet, almost pleading. He opened his mouth to speak, then dropped his hand, turned and walked across the porch.

She watched him walk across the yard. The dogs slept. The last chattering of lingering summer birds broke the soft autumn air. The pale sky stood out starkly against the deep green of the hickory leaves, and the mimosa, nearly dead from harsh winters, stood like a skeleton in the quickening breeze. Beside the porch, an unkempt rose bush spiraled upwards. The faint smell of wandering Jew and carnations wafted from the weedy flower garden. She turned and went back into the kitchen to finish her coffee. Rainwater turned to wave, but she had gone inside. Out back, the chickens cackled and the woman went out to prop the gate open so they could move about. Scattered clouds back-dropped the golden glow of corn in the field beyond the barn, the Howard's field. The woman stood beside the fence and gazed to where the trees became the sky.

Doom's Chapel

My girls, they'd be all grown now. 'Fraid I missed most of their growin' up, and for that, I am sorry. But sometimes, you can't stay. Sometimes, you have to pay a price and maybe nobody else knows what that price is but you. It makes it hard, though. Not being able to tell anyone. And not seeing your family.

I do miss them terribly though.

The cemetery nestled close to the bottom of a long, slow hill, partly hidden by great grey-barked hickories at the edge of the grounds and a scrub of cedars just outside what remained of the old, spiked iron fence. The markers, colored in drab pastels of yellow and green from years of lichen growth, absorbed heat from a late summer day. At one end of the old graveyard stood a weathered, peeling white chapel with a sign on it proclaiming it Doom's Chapel. No path led from the gravel road that passed nearby the cemetery.

Rainwater plodded down the hot, dusty grey lane. The just-beginning-to-set sun still glared down at him and into his eyes, and Rainwater cursed his mistake at trying to take a shortcut to the highway which led to his being lost now. He knew better than to get off the main road. This old gravel lane seemed to go on forever. He had figured this road would lead to the U. S. highway and from there it shouldn't be too difficult to catch a ride south, maybe as far as Tennessee, by night. But now it was clear the road only went farther and farther back into the country, and all Rainwater found along the way were fields of corn and cattle and, occasionally, a copse of trees hanging over the road where it bent to cross a creek by either ford or wooden bridge or to meander some long-forgotten property line. At least he had found water in a stream that appeared to be clean, but Rainwater couldn't be certain. There was always the chance that it flowed through a pasture upstream, or a field that had been sprayed with insecticide, but he had little choice. The day was hot. He was sticky from perspiration from his too heavy clothes and from lugging his pack, which seemed to weigh a hundred pounds in the moist-warm September air.

Rainwater had company as he walked: red wing black-birds sat on tufts of grass, barely bending the stalks, giving the white-headed traveler an "okalee!" as he trudged down the road; groundhogs fussed, hunched over some piece of digging and stood up to watch the old man pass; cows looked up slowly as he passed, watching with disinterested eyes, chewing slowly, steadily; lizards sunned themselves on the gravel of the road, scurrying off to the side and into the tall weeds as the traveler marched on. He had not seen any people along the road, not even a farmer working in a distant field. Now the light was beginning to fade and Rainwater wished for any sort of shelter to rest in for the night, but there were no barns or houses or sheds anywhere in sight.

Rainwater's stomach ached from hunger - he had not eaten since he had visited the soup kitchen at the Salvation Army in Greenville that morning - and now he would have to sleep outdoors. He tromped up a hill. He never should have taken a ride in the back of that farm truck. The farmer had let him out at the edge of nowhere and now he was lost someplace in far western Kentucky. He really had no idea where he might be. But any more, any ride was a relief, even one in the back of a dirty farm truck was better than walking, although he still had had to sit in the back while the farmer sat alone in the cab. There just wasn't any trust any more.

As he reached the top of the rise, he stopped and dropped his pack on the gravel. He reached down and grabbed a strap and dragged it off to the side, although he had seen no traffic since he had left Lamasco and made the mistake of taking this little road off into no place. He reached into his pack, took out a battered pack of cigarettes and lit a partially smoked butt. He hated spending what little money he had on cigarettes, but it was the one vice he allowed himself. He sat by the edge of the road, a little stand of trees behind him, and beyond that, yet more corn, and before him the road, winding on down the other side of the hill. He smoked his cigarette in the first dusky light of the beginning evening. A bright moon rose behind him, almost full. Rainwater turned and stared at the moon, dragging the smoke out of his cigarette. He stood up, dropped the spent butt onto the road and stepped on it. It was then he saw the tiny building at the bottom of the hill where the road turned and headed for still another creek.

Rainwater yanked up his bag and hustled stiffly down the road. If someone were home, he could perhaps find them just cleaning up after supper and glad to spare some leftovers with a man of the road. The light was beginning to fade more quickly now. Rainwater hurried to reach the bottom of the hill. He thought it odd that no lights came on in the house. When he walked around the turn in the road, the tiny structure appeared to be empty. He was disappointed, but decided at least he might find shelter for the night. Stepping now past the row of cedars that had partially hidden the building from his view, Rainwater stopped suddenly and dropped his bag again and stared at the little broken down chapel surrounded by an array of marble and granite markers leaning every which way and largely overgrown with Johnson grass and thistles. The sign hanging uneven above the door proclaimed it as Doom's Chapel. Doom's Chapel? Really? Truth in advertising, he supposed. Rainwater shook his head. The light was purple-grey now. Rainwater walked through the little cemetery, resigned to attempt to sleep within whatever protection the chapel might provide. He dragged his bag behind him. As he approached the site, stepping high over the weeds, his foot clanged on the remains of the old iron fence, twisted and destroyed by the extraordinary force that is a combination of time, rain, wind, sun, and disrepair. He was not excited about sleeping in a graveyard. It wasn't that he was superstitious - or at least he didn't consider himself superstitious - but he just didn't like the idea much. And Doom's Chapel? It just seemed a bit spooky.

When he walked past the first marker, he leaned over and read the inscription: Wm. Doom b. 1842 d. 1865 and below that in a small semicircle: SGT First Kentucky Brigade. Rainwater could barely read the words. They were washed out some and the dusky light made him need to kneel now before the marker to read it all. Clearly, it was a very old cemetery. And the name... He resolved to try to read some of the other stones, but after he had inspected the chapel.

Rainwater pushed on the fading wooden door, and it creaked but did not move much. He pushed it harder, moving it some, but something blocked the path the door would take. When he had pushed the door far enough, Rainwater slowly peered around the edge of the door until he could see in. It was almost dark, but he could see that the chapel was littered by the remains of an old pew, destroyed by vandals. There were chains and pieces of rope, perhaps used to place markers. What had blocked the door was a chunk of granite from one of the markers, broken off and hurled through the window perhaps by teenaged boys who saw the old chapel as an oddity and nothing more. Rainwater pushed the door harder and managed to open it enough to squeeze himself through. When he stepped in, a barred owl called loudly above him as it left the rafters and flew out through a hole at one end of the chapel, the suddenness of the sound making Rainwater's heart pound. The owl sat in one of the hickory trees at the edge of the cemetery and hooted at Rainwater for disturbing him. Inside the chapel, it was nearly dark, the windows being partially boarded up except for the one broken through by the slab of granite, but there was a spot in a corner that seemed clear enough to rest on. Rainwater scraped away pieces of debris and glass with his boot, then spread a frayed old blanket from his pack on the floor. It certainly wasn't the Hilton, but it would have to do.

Rainwater went back into the graveyard before it was totally dark and found a number of 1800 dates on the markers, and some markers that he couldn't quite decipher but might have been older. At one end of the cemetery was a long row of small stones each of which said, "Child." Some of them had dates and occasionally one would have a name but most of them did not. A huge red oak had grown up at one side of the cemetery. Beneath it were more markers with the names Doom and Curry on them. Rainwater walked around the graveyard and returned to the first marker he had seen. The last fading light fell on the stone, the angle of the light making the words easier to read. Rainwater thought there was a simple sacred look to the site. It seemed like a good place for an eternal rest. Rainwater wondered what sort of place he might end up. Some pauper's grave, perhaps. Or maybe tossed in a prison yard, if he was ever found. He shook his head to shake away the memory. He would prefer to be cremated and his ashes spread in the Pacific, where he had still so many memories of his early days in the merchant marines, his shipmates and he sharing adventures in ports from California to the Philippines. Then again, his girls were in Ohio. Ohio. One resting place is as good as another, he supposed. And in its way, it would have him close to his family. Rainwater realized he was kneeling and staring at the marker now.

"Well, Sergeant William Doom, may you rest in peace. You look to have come from a fine family." Rainwater's voice was swallowed up by the fading grasses and orange hickory leaves. He stood and nodded at the stone. "Sergeant," he said again. He had not heard a voice, even his own, all afternoon, and he let himself be kept brief company by the sound of it. A slow breeze brought cool air to Rainwater and he retreated to the chapel. As he squeezed into the door, the owl called from the hickory. Rainwater recalled his grandfather many years before telling him that the owls were always asking, "Who cooks for you?" He laughed and called to the bird, "Nobody cooks for me tonight." He pushed the door closed behind him and shoved the heavy piece of granite against the door to prevent any other animals from getting in. He curled up on the hard floor on his blanket, his limp overcoat still on, and fell into a quick, deep sleep. His long hike had drained him. Rainwater slept deeply, his tired muscles trying to relax after the long hike he had taken on the hot road. His leg muscles especially cried out for minerals to replace those lost to perspiration during the day. He was nearly dehydrated.

The owl roosted in a hickory tree, unwilling to fight the human for rights to the chapel.

It was nearly eleven when the pick-up truck pulled up next to the cemetery. Music was playing on the radio and a girl was giggling. Then the driver turned off the vehicle, opened his door, and climbed out. He walked quickly around the truck and opened the passenger door.

"Come on, Darlene. It's okay. My daddy used to take me out here rabbit huntin' when I was a kid. Ain't nobody comes out here no more, though. There ain't nothing to be scared of."

"Well, then why are you whisperin', Billy?" The girl giggled, but she was whispering too.

"Come on," the boy was pulling her hand. "Wait'll you see what I got fer you, Darlene." The boy reached into the back of the truck and grabbed a brown paper sack.

"Billy Doom, I know what you got," she laughed teasingly.

"Sshh." The boy put his finger to her lips and looked around himself in mock terror. "Don't you know they might hear you, and then they might GIT you." He jumped at her, and she giggled. Billy let go of Darlene's hand and reached into the back of the truck again, this time retrieving a small folded up white quilt. He trotted over to the cemetery. "Come on, Darlene." The girl climbed out of the truck and closed the door gently.

Darlene sat on the blanket next to Billy. She wore cutoffs and a thin white blouse.

"Here, try this, Darlene," Billy whispered. "It's called Morgan David. My momma drinks it all the time."

"Yore momma? I thought yore momma was a Baptist." Darlene laughed again. She took a long drink from the bottle. "Ooh, that's good, Billy. Here, you have some." She passed the bottle back to Billy, who took a long swig as well. "D'you steal this from yore momma?"

"Shoot no, Darlene, she'd beat me for drinkin', but she'd kill me for stealin' her drink." They both laughed quietly. "I got it from Johnny Jean. He has an I.D., you know."

"I don't like him." Darlene took another draw on the bottle. "He's always fightin' and tryin' to beat up on somebody. You oughtn't hang around with him." She drank again and passed the bottle back to Billy.

"Aw, he's okay. He's never messed with me." Billy took a drink from the bottle. The sweetness of the wine made him shudder. He gave it back to Darlene who swigged a drink.

"Ooh wee," she sighed. "I feel that goin' right to my head. If'n I didn't know better, I might think you had intentions,

Billy Doom." She said this louder and looked sideways at the boy in the moonlight, then lay flat on the blanket looking up at the stars. Billy watched her for a few minutes in the cool light of the moon and his eyes began to glaze over. "I just love the stars, Billy. Ain't they just too pretty?" she said after a few minutes. She propped herself up and took another long drink from the bottle. She handed the bottle back to Billy and lay back down as he swigged the wine.

"Yeah," Billy glanced skyward then returned to his stare at Darlene. The light from the moon accentuated her youthful figure and made soft her round, fair face.

"And the moon. Ain't it pretty too, Billy?" She sat up long enough to take another long drink. She had to turn it up high because they were already well into the bottle. She lay back down on the blanket and shivered. "I shoulda wore a sweater. If I'd known we were gonna sit out in the graveyard, I'd've wore a sweater." Billy watched her shiver, then leaned over suddenly and kissed her.

Rainwater felt the nudge of voices outside and stirred.

The owl on the hickory tree opened one eye, then the other. He turned his head and looked at the two humans lying next to the grave.

Rainwater's leg, his right leg, felt a definite, painful need for replenishment. It began to stiffen. Rainwater turned and rolled over near the small pile of ropes and chains.

"Oh, Billy, you take my breath away," Darlene whispered as she wrapped her arms around Billy's neck and kissed him. "Or maybe it's the wine." She giggled and kissed him again.

Billy pulled away for a moment. "Darlene, I want you," he said too flatly. Then he took another drink from the wine bottle. It was nearly empty now. Billy's head was beginning to spin. He reached down and placed his coarse hand on Darlene's chest and she moaned softly. Then she moved his hand from her breast to her side.

"Don't be a bad boy, Billy," she whispered.

"Come on, Darlene. Nobody'll know but you and me." Billy pressed his body on top of Darlene.

"Billy, no," she whispered. She kissed him again. "Let's just kiss."

"I don't wanna just kiss, Darlene. I want you." Billy pressed Darlene's shoulders to the ground.

"You're hurtin' me, Billy." Darlene called out and tried to free her arms.

"I don't wanna hurt you, Darlene. I wanna make you feel good, an' I wanna feel good myself." Billy held Darlene's arms close to her so that she couldn't move them. She struggled to push her arms outward with a firm and steady pressure.

"Billy, please don't do this. Please don't hurt me." Her voice was not gentle now, but firm and frightened and loud.

"Aw, come on, Darlene. You know you wanna as much as I do." He pressed himself on top of her and tried to kiss her, but she didn't want to kiss him now. He began to press his pelvis on Darlene. She struggled to free her arms, but he had her pinned.

"No, Billy! No! Stop!" She looked up at the marker they were lying beneath. "Oh," she said suddenly and Billy stopped pawing her for a moment. "Oh, my God, Billy!" Her eyes were fixed on the tombstone.

"What?" Billy pressed his hand on Darlene's breast again and began to move his hips on top of her.

Rainwater hobbled towards the door. He pulled it open, scraping the granite tombstone when he did.

"What was that?" Billy swiveled his head but he didn't move his body from atop Darlene.

Darlene squirmed under Billy's weight. "Billy, stop. You're hurtin' me. Wait. Look at that, Billy."

"What?" He groped around Darlene's zippered jeans, but he was too dizzy from the wine to figure out by feel what he should do.

"This is yore grave, Billy," Darlene said quickly, hoarsely. "This is yore grave!"

"What?" Billy looked up at the marker and saw his great-great uncle's name. "What?" he said louder.

Rainwater's leg cramped hard, but he was more concerned about the voices that now had him fully awake. He hobbled himself over to the broken window and peered out. He saw a girl – not much younger than his daughters - being held down by a boy, struggling. Rainwater's leg caught in one of the chains but he kept making his way outside the chapel to stop what was happening. Rainwater lurched out of the chapel, his cramped leg pulling the chain behind him, clanking. "Hey!" The moonlight made his grey coat ashen, his white hair glowing. He wanted to stop and free his leg, but he needed to stop this boy first.

His call surprised the owl and the owl let out a call from his perch in the tree.

"Billy!" Darlene's eyes grew wide. "Who's that?"

"Uhh!" Billy was already trying to stand up, but his balance was off and he staggered.

Rainwater's leg demanded potassium and cramped hard. He grabbed his cramping calf muscle and cried out in pain as he advanced on the two teenagers, the boy now tottering before him a head taller than he, "Aaah!" Rainwater started losing his footing and put both hands up to gain his balance "Aaaaah!" The pain was penetrating. He saw the girl, free from the boy, and he wanted her to get away before this oaf decided to beat up an old homeless man. "Go!" He yelled at the girl, but in the moonlight, his hands stretched before him, and his balance so off kilter, it really came out just towards the both of them. Billy backed up several steps, his eyes bugged out wide.

Darlene crawled a few feet on all fours before getting her feet up under her. She ran in a wine-induced zigzag towards the truck. Billy stumbled and fell on the old fence, his jeans snagging on the cast iron spikes.

The owl called again and flew to the red oak. Rainwater's foot finally untangled from the chain and he started falling forward towards Billy.

Darlene made it to the truck. "Come on, Billy!" she called impatiently. Billy was snared by the fence. He watched with terror as Rainwater stumbled towards him, out of control, landing directly on Billy's back.

"He's got me, Darlene! Oh Lord ha' mercy he's got me, Darlene! Oh, Momma!" Billy covered his eyes as Rainwater rolled off him. Rainwater worked to gain his footing, should there be a fight ensuing. His leg started to relax. Darlene saw the keys in the truck and drove off in a cloud of gravel and dust. Billy never turned around to face whatever had crawled out of the chapel after him. He finally freed himself from the fence and ran down the road after Darlene, his pants ripped from the crotch to the belt in the back. Darlene drove all the way to her house without slowing down. Billy ran for several miles before he finally slowed to a walk, then sat down in the road and threw up the half bottle of wine. Then he cried.

The moon was nearly set, its last light making the tombstones iridescent in the cool night air. Rainwater finally felt the muscle relax completely in his leg. He stood up straight. He looked at the route the young people had taken on their exit and shook his head. He turned around and picked up the white quilt and the almost empty bottle of wine. He looked down at the marker again. "Here's to you, Sergeant. There'll be no desecration tonight, sir." Rainwater drained the bottle and made his way back into the chapel and lay the quilt atop his other blanket. The owl flew back to the hickory tree and sat. Rainwater settled back on the floor to sleep. In the cemetery, a cricket began a slow, steady call.

The Bridge at Talbottsville

I've been all over the place and I'll tell you what: there's more good in folks than most folks know about. But there's also more bad in folks that we don't want to know. Even the most high and mighty town leader can have some dark thoughts, and, you know, thinking bad is pretty much the same as doin' bad, at least that's what I learned growing up. And the meanest person in town can end up doin' some of the kindest things you ever saw.

I knew a lady once in this little town in Missouri who never did talk to nobody and hardly ever even went out. Folks was scared of her, I think. Kids would run to the other end of the block if she came outside on her porch, which she didn't do much. Don't know anyone who would've said she was a nice person. Well, one day, she dies and they find out she's had all this money stashed in old bonds and such and she's left the lot of it to set up an animal shelter in her home town. Think of that. Taking care of all those strays. I'd say, that's a kind thing to do. Nobody ever saw it coming.

It wasn't much of a town. Rainwater had seen a few signs for Talbotsville, but when he trudged past one that read Talbotsville POP 1113, he didn't see much. If there wasn't more than this, he would need to move on.

The town consisted of a brick town hall/volunteer fire department, a hand-lettered sign on a wall dedicating it to Samuel Talbot. Beyond that, a wooden sidewalk covered by various metal awnings led to a hardware store, a consignment store, a drug store, and at the end, half underground, a pool hall and diner named The Dugout. What struck the old man most as he scuffed along the wooden sidewalk and peered into stores was there was not a soul around. In the drug store, a sign in the window said CLOSED SATURDAY, and below that SEE YOU AT THE BRIDGE! Across the street stood a darkened grocery, its parking lot's fading lines delineating where cars and trucks might park, except there were none.

Rainwater pressed his nose against the window of The Dugout. Inside was dark, except for an RC cola sign with "Our specialty: Bull-burger plate - $4.95 (thru the garden - $.45)." His mouth watered. He hadn't eaten since yesterday lunch. Since then, he had hitch-hiked and walked eighteen hours and several hundred miles. Now his stomach complained for his neglect of it. He walked towards a clump of houses down either side of the road and the lane that crossed it, hoping to find a benefactor, but the town appeared abandoned. Around a corner, he noticed a large, ornate steeple. Might as well test the charity of the church. He tried the door, but it was locked. It too had a sign: Come to the Bridge Saturday. There was a changeable letter sign next to the sidewalk that read: Prayer is Hand to Hand Combat. Rainwater wandered along the lane, turned down another side street, but saw no one. Another church huddled by a stream. He sighed and walked towards the simple brown spire.

Rainwater trudged along the chip-and-seal roadway. He still had seen no one. The church yard was empty except for a white picket fence protecting an array of weathered markers. He thought he smelled a fire, perhaps charcoal, maybe something cooking. He stepped up to the massive oak doors and tried the handle. To his surprise, the button depressed and the latch clicked. Pushing the door, he peered into the chamber.

"Hello? Anyone home?" He smiled at his unintended joke.

"Yes?" It was a tired voice, old, raspy. Rainwater stepped in, his eyes adjusting to the rich blue and red stained glass light that slathered over battered pews and fading carpet. The room was unlit otherwise. The window scene depicted a brown-bearded Jesus in the garden, resting against a boulder, his red robe draped about him, a single ray of heavenly light drawing his blue eyes upward. A brass plaque engraved with Geo. Talbot was barely visible below it. Up three steps at the end of the room stood a dark pulpit and before it a figure in his alb, his back to the pews, head bowed. The church returned to its quiet. Finally, without turning, the preacher raised his head. "Why aren't you at the bridge?" He paused, then turned and faced Rainwater. "You still here?"

"Yes, sir." Rainwater stepped forward, but it was no lighter than where he had stood a moment before. "I'm here."

The preacher walked with familiar, measured paces down the steps and up the aisle. "You shouldn't be out if you're not going down to the bridge, you know. They said everyone had to go. I don't care if they do anything to me, but you've got to be careful." The preacher stared beyond Rainwater.

"I don't know about all that. I'm new to town. Just came by looking for work. I'm hungry and tired. I need help. Folks know me as Rainwater." He struck up a sincere and needy posture. The preacher maintained his stare. He walked towards

Rainwater, stopping well short. It was only then that Rainwater saw his glassy, blind eyes. "Oh," Rainwater said involuntarily.

The minister chuckled. "Guess I should wear sunglasses for the benefit of others, but seems to me, those are my sunglasses." He pointed with his thumb towards the stained-glass window. "I'm Brother Zoener." He didn't offer his hand, but was too far away for Rainwater to take his hand anyway. "Drifter, huh?"

Rainwater nodded.

The old preacher stood quietly. "You just passing through then?"

"Yes, sir. On my way south, saw the signs for the town and . . ."

"And thought you were coming someplace, huh?" The preacher laughed. "Listen, Rainwater, take my advice and head out. Nothing going on in this God-forsaken little town to help a stranger. In fact, this town doesn't take well to strangers. I'd leave myself if I could." He turned and retreated towards the pulpit.

Rainwater shook his head. "There any place I might find some food?" He tried to transfer the sincere, needy posture to his voice. "There a cookout or something at the bridge? Maybe I could get food there?" The minister stopped.

"No. No, don't go to the bridge. I'll find you something to eat. Come with me." He walked up the steps, passed the pulpit, and felt along a back wall, opening a door and motioning to Rainwater. "Come with me."

Rainwater followed him into the dark room, tripping over a small table. He sat down suddenly to keep from falling.

"Sorry. Switch is next to the door. Never think about it, you know." Brother Zoener removed his robe and draped it on a cot. Rainwater could see the sleeves of his shirt were rolled up to his elbows. He rustled in a cabinet in the dark. Rainwater could just make out his silhouette.

"So what's going on at the bridge?" Rainwater stood, flipped the switch and was blinded by florescent light. When his eyes adjusted, he saw his host's chambers, spare and neat: a cot, a little kitchen, a couple of tables and chairs. That was it. No pictures, no rugs and no disorder.

"There's nothing going on. They're having a cookout, like you said." The preacher didn't turn or raise his voice, but sounded vaguely sarcastic. He prepared a sandwich.

"Then why shouldn't I go?" Rainwater pressed, but not so hard as to ruin his opportunity for food. He sat in a chair and watched the back of the frail figure hunched over the counter.

"Folks 'round here just not given to newcomers, is all." The preacher placed a plate with a bologna sandwich, two pickles, and a small mound of potato chip crumbs on the table. "Here. Eat this, then leave the way you came."

Rainwater bit into the sandwich. "Where's the road go south?"

Zoener chuckled, softer this time. "Nothing south of Talbotsville. The road goes on a couple miles past the bridge then stops before the Old Place. There's no other houses, just the Old Place. Well, and no bridge either, now."

"Old place?" Rainwater bit into a homemade pickle, its sourness tightening his jaws.

"The old Talbot place. Folks here abouts call it the Old Place." The preacher sat, hands folded on the table. "Sandwich okay?"

"Tasty, quite tasty. Course, you know the saying: hunger makes the best sauce." Rainwater swallowed. "Is that 'the old Talbot place' as in Talbotsville?"

"It is." Reverend Zoener stood. "I forgot. You'll need something to drink." He reached in the cabinet, felt for an old jar and filled it with water. He placed it in the middle of the table. "Forgive the glass. I break glasses, sometimes. These are cheaper and easier to come by."

Rainwater ate a stale chip. "Talbots must be important folks. Name's on everything; the fire station, the window in there, even the town itself." Rainwater sipped cool, metallic water.

"Oh yeah." The old man returned to his chair. "The Talbots were the richest folks in town. They helped this town a lot. Folks forget how much they helped." He shook his head.

"They pay for the fire station?"

The preacher nodded. "Fire station. Paved the streets back when they were just dirt and gravel. Why, they even got the steeple for the Baptists. But folks don't think about that. All they think about is that bridge. Seems no one forgets about the bridge."

"What about the bridge?" Rainwater finished the chips and scooted the plate.

The preacher rose and felt for the plate. "The Talbots paid for the bridge, too." He said it as if that was it.

"Why would anybody care if they built a bridge? They live over there, right? Isn't that where you said the Old Place is?" Rainwater finished off the water and the minister took the glass.

"Well, they loaned the town the money for the bridge, actually. I mean, a bridge is expensive. Nobody could expect them to pay for the whole bridge themselves, could they?"

"Nice bridge?"

"Oh yeah, beautiful bridge, all stone and mortar, just like you'd see in Paris or someplace. Folks oughta be proud of it, instead of making all that fuss."

"Why'd they build a fancy bridge if the road stops? Seems like any old bridge would do if you're just talking about being local."

The reverend snorted, "Huh. You sound like the rest of them." Steam rose in the sink.

"That what people upset about? Because they built a fancy bridge that didn't go any place? Why build it then?"

"Well, it was supposed to go someplace. When they built the bridge, there was talk of the road going on over to Wildersville. From there, it's not far to Lexington. Folks thought the road would make this little town into something. I guess they thought being a big city was a good thing. Me, I like it better this way. Or I did. Not much to like any more about this town." He dried the jar with a tattered tea towel.

"If you don't like it here, why don't you leave?"

The minister snorted a laugh. "Leave? Where would I go?"

"Same place I'm going?" Rainwater shrugged. "Head down the road. I got no one to report to, no place I gotta go."

"That make you happy?"

"Happy? Never think about being happy. It's just life."

"It's your life, maybe." The preacher nodded towards the table where Rainwater's voice came from. "But you might've made any number of choices different, couldn't you?"

"Maybe. But 'knowing how way leads onto way' and all that." Rainwater felt a little cornered.

"No regrets?" The minister pressed.

"Yeah, plenty." Rainwater pushed the thought of his daughters out of his mind. And his friend. He shook the thought out of his head. "But the road works for me now."

"I'm sure it does, Rainwater." The minister lightened his tone. "But I'm not you. Wouldn't that be a sight? A drifter and an old blind preacher heading down the road?" The preacher stared towards the door.

"Well, I guess you're right. Seems like you have a heavy burden, Reverend."

The minister leaned backwards against the countertop and wiped his hands absent-mindedly on the dishtowel. "So tell me something, Rainwater. Where'd you sleep last night?"

Rainwater shrugged. "Out on the road."

"And where will you sleep tonight?"

Rainwater smiled. "Same place."

The minister nodded. "When you leave here, you're going home." He turned and ran a soapy cloth over the plate and rinsed it in running water.

"Yeah, I guess. Such as it is."

"And this is my home, Rainwater, such as it is. I've lived here forty years. I know everybody in this town, can still see their faces. They're good people, really, on the inside. It's just that bridge and . . ." The preacher leaned wearily on the sink. "If ever my flock needed me, . . ."

"I see what you mean, brother. But what happened to the road? Why doesn't it go anywhere? Why'd they build that fancy bridge to no-where?"

The preacher snickered. "Oh yeah, the road. It goes out to the Old Place and stops. The Talbots wouldn't sell the land to build the road, so it just stops there in front of their house. They tied it up in the courts and never did get it resolved. On the other side, they built the road from Wildersville, but had to stop when they got the Talbot's too, so it just stops over on the other side of the field. At one time, you could see both ends of the road from the Old Place, but they never connected them. Then they came and put the interstate in. Don't guess they could connect them now if they wanted to. The Talbots didn't want to sell for that either, but of course, they don't ask, they tell." He replaced the dishes in the cabinet and sat down.

"Well, it does sound kind of bad. Rich folks get the town to build a bridge that just goes to their house."

"Talbots financed it. But I guess that's part of it. The Talbots got even richer from that. And they had to name the town after them. Used to be called Riverside. Lots of people didn't take kindly to that, but figured it was worth it if we became a big city. Folks sure got tired of seeing Miss Edith in her old Cadillac, driving around like she owned the place, partly because I guess she did." The preacher shrugged. "But she spent her money in town. If it was the folks' own money, at least they were getting it back, after a fashion."

"Miss Edith, she a Talbot?"

"Yeah, last one. Never married. Folks said anyone who came courting on her was run out of town. They didn't want any more Talbots." He shook his head.

"How old's Miss Edith?" Rainwater stood to leave.

"Miss Talbot died last Sunday." The preacher frowned.

"Oh, I'm sorry."

"Me too. But I guess we're about the only ones." He started for the door and Rainwater picked up his pack. "But I never thought they'd do this." Brother Zoener led him across the podium and down into the church.

"So what are they doing, sir?"

"They're tearing up the bridge, Rainwater. Taking it apart stone by stone, leaving the rocks at the edge and nobody'll be able to go across."

"What about the Old Place? How will anyone get over there?" Rainwater opened the oak door and squinted in the sunlight.

"Gone. They burned it Monday. Bunch of kids I guess. A pity, really. So much history, so much of our history, gone. But nobody cares. Nobody even asked about it. To tell the truth, I think folks were glad. But now this." The old minister shook his head, the sunlight showing his pallid, drawn skin.

Rainwater tugged his pack up his shoulder. "Well, thank you, Reverend. Guess I will go the other way. No sense going to a cookout if folks don't want you there." He waved, then realized his error. "Good luck," he called too loudly. Rainwater took a couple of steps, then turned again. "You burying Miss Edith in the courtyard?"

"No, Rainwater, there's nothing to bury. Go on now. Go on down the road and forget about Talbotsville. It's not a very good place."

Rainwater smelled smoke and heard a roar go up from a crowd, their voices carried down the river. "Nothing to bury?"

"I'm going inside. I'm going to pray and thank God I am blind, that I cannot see how evil my town, my neighbors, my friends have become. I closed my eyes to the hatred. I have my reward." He started back in the dark church. "Good luck, Rainwater. Travel quickly and with God's grace."

Rainwater watched him pull the door open. "Why is there nothing to bury, Reverend?"

The old man turned, his sightless eyes unfocused. "They're not having a cookout, Rainwater. That's Miss Edith's flesh you smell. They're burning her. They've burned the Old Place and now they're burning poor old Edith. I'm told they plan to toss her ashes in the river. Go on now Rainwater. Go someplace that has a soul." Rainwater heard the door slam behind him as he turned and walked through town. He imagined the preacher back inside his church, kneeling, praying. He hurried past the sign that read Talbotsville POP 1113.

I Am a Good Man

*Once I was in San Diego and we all got real drunk on cheap wine,
a bunch of fellas and me. Lord, we were plastered. One of the guys
decided we should all go down and get tattoos, because we were
in the merchant marines and we ought to be proud of it. Well, at
first everyone is kind of scared to, so we drink some more wine to
get our courage up. Well, I got so drunk, I passed out and when
I wake up, everybody's gone. I waited around for a while then I
went out, I was still drunk, and I see the whole lot of them coming
down the street and they're all comparing tattoos and looking real
proud of themselves. They had ships and eagles and anchors, girls
names and "Mom" and just about anything else you could imagine
all over them. One fella had a big American flag with an eagle
perched on top. Took up his whole arm, just about. Well, first I
was real mad cause they'd gone off and left me and I didn't have
a tattoo, but then we started sobering up and some of the guys
started looking at their arms like they wished they hadn't done it,
and then I was kind of glad I'd passed out. That was when I was
seventeen. I'd lied about my age to get into the merchant marines.*

The heavy old station wagon swayed on the wet highway, sending a spray on the cars behind that in turn sent sprays on the cars behind them. The gold-colored lights on the bank sign read; eight seventeen, forty degrees, eight seventeen. The sky was grey, but the rain had stopped. The car radio played Christmas music. It was the day after Thanksgiving. The wipers flipped off the spray from the cars ahead. To the side, a man with a rumpled raincoat leaned over the road, his thumb out. The driver of the station wagon pulled over, reached over to the passenger seat and tossed a notebook into the back seat. The hitch hiker ran up and opened the back door of the wagon. He threw his duffle bag onto the floor in the back then climbed in the front. The driver suppressed his concern for the carpet in the back. It was a company car anyway.

"Thanks for the lift. It's getting kinda nasty out there." The hitchhiker pulled off his wet hat and long white curls dripping with rain fell around his face. He brushed his hair back with his free hand.

"Where you heading?" the driver asked, carefully watching the road and his rider at the same time.

"South. Mind if I smoke?" He pulled a pack of Camels out of his pocket and held them up to confirm his request.

"Nah, go ahead."

The hitchhiker lit a cigarette then pulled out a thin sheeted Bible from the pocket of his rumpled, stained coat and started reading. The driver watched the road and occasionally glanced at the old man with long grey-blond hair and white whiskers next to him. He felt uneasy in the silence. He had wanted someone to talk with on his drive. That was a part of the reason for picking him up, that, and the fact that it was the holidays and no one should be stranded in the rain during the holidays. "You a preacher?"

The old man looked up sideways at the driver. "Because I'm reading the Good Book? No sir, I just like to read it. It gives me some comfort sometimes, you know?"

The driver did not want to talk about the Bible. He wanted something lighter to talk about. "Where you coming from?"

"Clarksville, through Nashville," the hitchhiker said, folding up his Bible and replacing in his pocket. "Thought I might find some work in the warehouses, but everybody's laying men off now. I can do lots of things still but I guess I'm too old for anyone to hire. Got a bad back anyway. Slept on a grate last night but it's getting too cold and too hard for these tired old bones to sleep outdoors anymore. Thought I'd head south for the winter, like the birds." He chuckled softly, under his breath. "By the way, folks call me Rainwater," he said without looking at the driver. He paused, as if waiting for the name to settle on the driver.

"Mine's Mark. Glad to meet you," the driver wanted to extend his hand for a handshake, but it seemed awkward in the car.

"Well, Mark, I gotta tell you, I've been all up and down these highways," Rainwater began. "Strange how you always go back. I've been to Florida a dozen times and now, I guess I'll go back down to Florida, maybe pick fruit this time." He took a long draw on his cigarette. "Never done that before." He rolled down the window an inch. "But there's a first time for everything." He knocked the ashes from his cigarette through the crack in the window. "Look at all the people on the road. Thought it was a holiday." He looked out the window at the passing trees.

"For some, I guess," said the driver. "Me, I'm on the highway, too. Salesman." He said it proudly. "I don't much care for it on the holidays much, but it's a living. It can get a little lonely sometimes, but I guess you know what I mean, huh, Rainwater? Spent Thanksgiving on a grate, huh? That's tough." He shook his head. Rainwater looked over at the driver, his eyebrows raised. "Silver Bells" began playing on the radio.

"Tough? Na, it ain't tough. Ain't nothing so tough any more. I mean, I got folks I coulda stayed with up in Ohio, but I decided not to. There's no sense butting in on them. I don't suppose they'd much wanna see me anyways, but they woulda put me up. Maybe." He lowered his head. He looked up again quickly, as if avoiding the gloom. "But I'm heading south now. It'll be great down south. You ever go crabbing?" The driver shook his head. "It's easy. Old black man named Albert showed me how one time using a chicken wing and a piece of string. A little patience and you can have all the crab you want." He forced a little laugh. "Yeah, maybe that's what I'll do. Sure can't sleep on the road anymore, what with the weather and all." He slid the cigarette butt through the partially open window and rolled it shut. "But heck, enough about me. Tell me about yourself. A salesman, huh? What do you sell?"

"Copper," said the driver. "Bulk copper. You know, to big industries around. Business isn't too bad, but copper's up right now so some people are holding off, waiting for it to go down."

"Yeah, seems like everything is higher than a cat's back anymore," broke in Rainwater. "Makes it tough on us poor working slobs, huh?" He looked at the driver for support but did not let him answer. "Yeah, maybe I'll go to Florida and pick fruit or vegetables. Gotta start somewhere. Maybe get a stake and start my own handyman business. Now that'd be nice."

The driver nodded. "Yeah, a good handyman can do okay. It's a good business. Me, I'm a college man. Got a degree in art history. Don't know what I ever thought I'd do with that."

He shrugged and laughed softly. "Kind of a waste I guess," he trailed off. "But you know," he started again, "I wouldn't trade those days for anything. Best years of my life. Heck, I had a date with a different girl every other night." He stuck out his elbow to nudge Rainwater, but he was sitting too far away. "And the parties, oh, man." He chuckled softly to himself.

"College man, huh? That's good. College is a good thing. Makes people think more, I'd say. An education, there's something you always got." Rainwater looked at the driver who was still smiling about his college days. "My wife went to college. She didn't finish, but she went, and then we had the girls. Now they were smart. I'll bet they were about as smart as anyone. Yeah, I remember when they were just tykes, they would make up stories, and..."

"You had breakfast?" the driver interrupted.

"No sir, 'fraid I don't have the money for breakfast."

"My treat." The driver pulled off the highway into a parking lot. The sign read: Blue Bell Diner. And under that it said: Breakfast Twenty-Four Hours. There were several large trucks in the gravel lot as well as a half dozen cars.

Inside, it was bright and clean. The smell of coffee and fresh biscuits filled the room. Three large, tired-looking men were sitting by the door. A family sat in one corner. Two men in suits sat at a table in the middle of the room. One had his briefcase open to the side and some papers spread upside down before him so the other man could read them. Two middle-aged women were at the table in the corner where the large, steamy windows met. The register jingled as a man with a tooth pick in his mouth and another man walked out past Rainwater and his benefactor. Rainwater started suddenly at the sight of the man. He looked familiar just for a second. But Rainwater knew it wasn't him.

"Y'all come back," said the dowdy woman behind the counter, but she did not look up at the men. She was sorting coins into the register drawer.

Rainwater and his host sat by a large window overlooking the gravel lot. The woman from the cash register brought over water and menus. "What's the best thing you got?" The salesman leaned back and did not look at the menu. The woman turned over cups that had been upside down on their saucers and poured coffee.

"Well, depends on what you like." She dropped tableware wrapped in napkins beside the two men. "But I make the biscuits and gravy myself." Now she stood proudly next to the table, one hand on her hip, the other holding up the coffee pot.

"Sounds great to me, and a rasher of bacon with two eggs up. How 'bout you, Rainwater." He found he liked saying his name.

"I'll have the same." He picked up his cup and drank long and slowly. The hot, bitter coffee warmed him and he felt suddenly safe as the man who had just paid got into his pickup truck and drove away. Rainwater looked out the window and shook his head. "You know, you were talking about going to college. Sometimes I think it's a shame 'bout young folks nowadays. I mean, what the hell they got to look forward to anymore? They can go to college, but that doesn't mean they'll get jobs when they get out. They can work all the time and still not be able to buy a house anymore. They can have families and never get to see them. I tell you, it'd be tough be young nowadays. As old and beat up as I am, I don't envy you much."

The salesman was not real sure he liked the vaguely condescending tone he heard coming from a tramp he had picked up hitch hiking. "Well, it's not so bad really. There's lots of opportunity if you know where to look for it. I never really thought

I'd be a salesman, but it's okay. I'm not complaining. I make a decent salary, got a company car, and that's okay. We got a nice apartment with a pool for the complex. Yeah, I'm doing okay."

"I'm sure you are, young fella. I didn't mean nothing by it. I'll bet you're a good man."

The salesman looked up from his coffee when Rainwater said it. It sounded funny to him, like something from a different era. "Well, yeah, I guess I am. Sure. I try to be, anyway. I was top producer in the region last quarter. That's doing a good job, isn't it?" He shrugged and smiled at Rainwater.

"Sounds like it. You married?" Rainwater did not look up. He was intent on his coffee.

"Yeah, sure am. Got a little boy, too. Cutest kid you ever wanted to see."

"You ever miss 'em. I mean when you're out on the road and all?" Rainwater let his mind wander to his own children and their children, at least, the last time he had seen them.

"Yeah, sure, sometimes. But I travel five days, then I'm in the office for four days then I'm off two. So I get to see them pretty much."

"What's your boy's name?" Rainwater cut off his own recollection.

The salesman was finished with his coffee and was looking for the waitress, holding his coffee cup next to his face. "Mark Junior."

"Bet he's a good boy, too."

"Oh yeah, he's a great kid. And smart, too. You know, he's only five and he can read up a storm. My wife was telling me on the phone last night that one of the books she just got for him, he can already read it."

Rainwater looked up at the young salesman, smiled and nodded. "Huh! That's real good, alright. What book was it?"

"Oh, I don't know. It's one of those rhyming books she says he likes. Yeah, she's all the time buying him books." He looked down at the table where the waitress had slid the two plates in front of him. She went to the other side and slid Rainwater's plates in front of him. Then she hurried off for the coffee pot. "You know, I ought to buy him one of those books while I'm in Murphreesboro." He paused. "Well, no, I guess I won't. I don't really know which ones he's already got." The salesman picked up his fork, but he did not use it right away. He looked past Rainwater, at nothing in particular, slowly twirling the steel fork in his hand.

Rainwater was using a half biscuit to sop up egg yolk on his plate. He pointed with his fork. "You'd better eat up. It'll get cold."

"Yeah." The young man began to eat, slowly at first, then faster.

Rainwater shoved a forkful of biscuit with a healthy dollop of gravy on it into his mouth. The rich, hearty, salty flavor was warm and satisfying. He had not eaten for two days, so he ate very deliberately. It tasted too good, and, besides, he had no idea how long it might be before his next meal. Then he had a memory and looked up at the young man across from him. "I remember one time I was stranded for the whole Thanksgiving weekend. Little town named Cricket Corner. Not really even a town, I guess," he waved with his fork. "Had maybe ten people in the whole town. One man was the mayor, police chief, and tax collector, all in one. I got stranded there one night and he let me sleep on the floor of his bar for the night and I ended up staying the whole weekend. He was a good man, too. Worked hard, like you. He had a store, a bar, and a gas station, all right there in Cricket Corner. His whole family worked hard. One son was the bar tender, another pumped gas. His daughter worked at the store, and so on. Yeah, if you stopped at in Cricket Corner, you stopped at his place and you met his family." Rainwater returned to the plate of food in front of him.

The salesman had stopped eating now and he sat there, his coffee cup in one hand, and watched the old man eat. That's twice he's used that phrase, a good man. Yeah, I guess I am a good man. Hadn't the regional manager told him that just the other day? That's why he'd been sent on this trip. He was supposed to be off this week, but the sales were way off in the region and he'd been sent to Murphreesboro to try to help out. I am a good man: the best the company's got, he thought. He watched the butter melting on his grits. He replaced his cup in its saucer and picked up his fork slowly. He cut an egg yolk and the yellow bled out onto the plate. Rainwater was scraping the last of the gravy out of the bowl with his fork.

"So, where'd you spend Thanksgiving?"

"What do you mean?" The salesman raised his eyebrows to look up at the old man without moving his head.

"Well, you said you spoke to your wife on the phone. I figured you must have been on the road."

"Yeah, well, I stayed in a motel near Bowling Green. I needed to get an early start on my appointments and all. But I'll be getting home next week." He looked intently at Rainwater. Rainwater called the waitress over for more coffee.

"You want some too?'

"Well, maybe a half a cup." The salesman wiped his mouth. "Listen, I've got to go on in to Murphreesboro. I've got clients to call on, and all."

"Oh sure, I understand. But really, thanks for breakfast. It tasted awfully good." Rainwater patted his stomach. "Yeah, I should be able make it down to Georgia by night time, out run the snow, and then I'll be doin' fine." He smiled broadly.

"Yes sir, thanks a load. It's folks like you make me feel good about the human race. I said it before and I'll say it again; you're a good man. That company's real lucky to have a fellow like you." He paused a second then finished the coffee in his cup. "Well, I'd better hit the road if I'm to make Georgia by dark. Travellin' man can't let the moss grow under his feet, can he?" He got up and wiped his mouth at the same time. "Thanks again," he called as he walked towards the door. His leaving seemed awkward, abrupt. The salesman waved and Rainwater walked away through the door and across the parking lot to the station wagon. He dragged his duffle out of the back seat of the station wagon then started up the ramp to interstate twenty-four. The salesman watched him walk, then lean out to the cars as they passed, his thumb out, then turn and walk after they had passed. After Rainwater had walked halfway up the ramp, he stopped, put his bag down, arched his back and pushed a knuckle into his back. The salesman was watching Rainwater walk when the sound of a news-paper rack broke his reverie. He turned and saw the boy who was having trouble getting the rack open so he could get his father a paper. His father went over to the rack impatiently and yanked it open then returned to his table with the paper. The boy followed his father to the table and was asking him a question, but the father hadn't heard. The salesman looked back out the window and Rainwater was still leaning out to the cars that passed on the ramp. Funny, he thought, who we meet. That old man and me, we don't have a thing in common. Not a thing. Me, I'm working steady, never late. I've got folks who count on me.

"Think it'll snow?" The boy's voice broke into his thoughts. It was the little boy who had tried to buy the paper for his father. Now his father looked over his paper.

"Danny, get over here and leave that man alone," the father barked at the boy. The father shook his head at the salesman as if to share some secret about how children get into trouble.

The salesman had wanted to answer. He had wanted to say, "It's okay" or "Yeah, the weatherman said it might snow as much as five inches by night time," but the boy was gone, sitting quietly at the table with his father who was reading the paper again. The boy looked expressionless at the salesman, then looked away. He sat very still. The salesman got up from the table and dropped a couple of singles next to his plate. The register jingled as he paid his tab.

"Y'all come back now," the woman did not look up, but dropped the coins into their slots and slid the bills into their places.

When the salesman went out into the parking lot, he looked up and Rainwater was still there, on the highway now, leaning out to the cars. The salesman looked back at the restaurant and he could see the boy inside, watching him with that same even look through the window. When he started the big station wagon, the radio was playing "Blue Christmas." The salesman reached into the back seat and picked up the notebook he had tossed there. He had an appointment at ten thirty. He could just make it. If he left that minute and went straight into town, he would be right on time. His regional manager had always said punctuality was very important, and he had always made a point of being on time. "A good salesman is always on time," was Mark's motto. He closed his notebook and drummed his fingers on the cover. Finally, he tossed the notebook on the passenger seat and said aloud, "Hell, I'm going home. I'm a better man than that." When he turned the car around in the parking lot, the salesman looked again, but Rainwater was not in sight. The man on the radio said it would snow as far south as Atlanta. It began to rain.

The Christmas Letter

I got folks. Everybody's got folks somewhere, I guess. Some people just get to see their kin more often that they like, some not often enough. Either way, seems like everybody complains about their folks sometime or another.

It was snowing again. The streets were already covered with the grey black slush from yesterday's snow and exhaust from the morning traffic, and now it was snowing again. The streets were full of dirty cars, packed together, moving slowly. Heavy trucks spewed stale sweet diesel fumes. People crowded along the sidewalk, walking quickly with their arms full of bags, occasionally jostling each other but seemingly without notice. The store windows flashed green, red, yellow. One had a moving mannequin dressed like Santa Claus alternating between picking up his bag and waving to the passersby. On the corner, a thin, tired Santa rang a bell beside a tripod where a bucket hung.

Rainwater hunched his shoulders against the wind that blew in where the buttons were missing in the middle of his coat. He walked close to the buildings. "I should have gone South like I planned," he muttered. He wouldn't mind the snow, if he didn't have to be out in it. He tried to enjoy watching the people pass at Christmas time, but the cold made his nose run. He shuffled stiffly around a small group of people huddled before a store. He shook his head at the wide-eyed look in the children's eyes as they pointed to the store window where yet another Santa held yet another child on his lap. Rainwater pushed along the edge of the crowd, trying hard to appreciate the lights and the muffled mix of music which drifted on the brittle air from the stores and from speakers along the sidewalk. Rainwater tried to like Christmas, but it was just so cold.

He walked with short, stiff steps along the busy boulevard, watching the shoppers and looking in the windows, until the stores turned into offices. He crossed the street and walked back. It was better with the wind at his back, but he was still cold. He turned a corner down a narrow side street. There were only a few stores on this street, mostly pawn shops and darkly painted grocery stores with foreign letters on the windows and strange smells drifting from the doors when people went through. He stepped in an icy puddle, soaking his worn boots through to his socks, but he didn't stop. After a couple of blocks, he walked into a doorway where a sign read: Bayview Hotel. From there, he could not see the bay. Rainwater opened the door to the hotel and climbed up the flight of stairs, walked slowly down a dim hall and up another flight, pulling heavily on the bannister with each step. He stopped before a door and leaned against the wall to catch his breath. The hallway was narrow. Small chunks of plaster from the ceiling peppered the yellowing linoleum before the door. Rainwater tapped his foot softly to relieve the numbness in it. His hip ached. He worked his cold fingers into his pocket, pulled out a key, and opened the door.

The small room absorbed a pale light from the window. Out the window were the rooftops of warehouses and garages. Rainwater flipped the dirt-stained switch by the door and the bare light bulb hanging from the ceiling cut deep shadows along the ceiling and the walls. He sat on the small bed, its meager springs squeaking, and looked at the battered little table in the corner, not because it interested him, but because it was the only other piece of furniture in the room. He looked over to where a sink stood in the other corner, then back to the anemic green wall opposite the bed where a torn shower curtain served as a door for what functioned as the closet, a triangular space beneath where the stairs went on up to the fourth floor. The room cost five dollars a night and he had been there for three weeks. The air was too dry and warm and the glare of the light made it seem even hotter in the room, but it was far better than the cold and wet outdoors. He stood up and took his damp coat off and dropped it over the steel foot of the sagging bed.

He reached in his pocket and pulled out some bills and coins. He still had thirty dollars from when he had worked by the dock sweeping straw from a warehouse. That ought to last through next Thursday, he figured, then he would need to move on. He sat back on the bed and the metal frame groaned. Next Thursday was Christmas. Well, maybe that would be good. Folks would be out on the highway on Friday, going home or back on the road to their jobs. Of course, families wouldn't pick him up, but sometimes truckers would, or maybe a lonely salesman out on the road. That's what he'd do. He would hitch a ride south on Friday after Christmas. January was no time to be in the city. It's cold and there's no work.

Rainwater pulled off his boots and swung his damp feet up on the bed, his arms behind his head as a pillow on top of the hard pillow that was provided. He stared out the window at the grey rooftops and the slow, steady snowfall. He thought about how many of those children he'd seen out on the street looking into the store windows would wake up to a cold, lonely house next Thursday and their deep, unspoken disappointment, only to get fed the same stories and go through the whole thing again next year. The idea made him scowl. He remembered telling his own children ridiculous stories of Santa Claus. It's just what they did. Then, of course, they had already stopped believing long before he had left. He wondered what they did believe in. They would be, what? In their twenties? Or, no, older still. How long had it been? But it wouldn't be that long before they'd perpetuate the game on their own children. Maybe they already had children. Maybe Rainwater was a grandfather. Rainwater wagged his head slowly as he watched the wind-blown flakes fly sideways in the darkening air across the window. He tried to picture what his grandchildren might be like, but the image wouldn't come, staying just out of focus for him. He focused on his daughters instead, picturing them all grown up, shopping in the big malls out in the subdivisions where they probably lived, fighting traffic, running to stores on their lunches, frantically searching for just the right gifts. He chuckled a short "Huh" just to think of it. Maybe they were going to see their mother for Christmas. They probably went to Grandmother's house. Well, he guessed she'd like that. She'd probably take them skating down at the rink the day after Christmas like they had when he and she were youngsters themselves. He supposed there still was a rink there. Maybe not. It was a complicated picture, his daughters with faces that had somehow not aged, his wife hopefully having moved on, maybe even grandchildren. And sons-in-law, and houses and cars and so much he could not fill in.

Of course, whether or not they spent Christmas with Grandmother depended on how far it was from his daughters' homes. When he had left, of course, they all lived in Ohio, but he had no way of knowing now. He had not seen his daughters in all these years. Maybe there were lots of grand-children now. He smiled now at the thought of it. There was a good chance of that. He wondered what they had been told over the years about him, about their grandfather. Maybe they never spoke about him or perhaps they even thought he was dead. He might as well be, for all they would know. Maybe it was better if they thought he was dead. If anyone asked about him, they could just say he was gone. Actually, that was true, he supposed. And what would the kids' Grandma say about him? That wouldn't be a pretty thought. Then again, perhaps not. She had been the forgiving sort, really, if she were even still alive. Rainwater shivered at the thought and tried not to think about the possibility. He sighed deeply and returned to the image he had made of his daughters. He really ought to write to them. He ought to write to his daughters and tell them that he was all right and that he was thinking about them and he hoped they would have a nice Christmas.

"I think I'll do that," he said aloud. His voice echoed slightly in the quiet room. Rainwater swung his feet off the bed, stood up and crossed to the table. The drawer was swollen and off track, but he managed to yank it open. In the drawer, he found a yellowing piece of paper that he pulled out and put on the table. In his bag, under the stairs, he found a plastic ballpoint pen advertising a loan company. He had found the pen ironic when he picked it up, but he had kept it just the same. He leaned over the table and wrote deliberately.

> Dear Sandy,
>
> It's almost Christmas and I thought I'd write to say I'm fine. I hope you are doing okay too. I'll stop by when I get to Ohio. Merry Christmas.
>
> Love,
> Papa

Rainwater folded the letter and put it in his shirt pocket. He would go to the library and find his daughter's address on a computer there. If he mailed it tomorrow, it might get there before Christmas. He lay back on the bed again and stared out the window. The snow was still falling but the wind had slowed to an occasional gust.

Rainwater watched it snow. Each flake looked as if it fell in a separate space, alone, until it piled up atop the sill outside the window. He felt his eyes moisten. He remembered back to the Christmases when he was a child; the warm house smelling of turkey and pies on Christmas eve; his Mom and Dad and all the adult relatives laughing and singing loudly and off-key as they sat before the needle-shedding Christmas tree drinking bitter smelling drinks, staring at the large, colored bulbs; his father working his way along the string of lights, tightening the bulbs, thwacking them with his finger so the lights would glow; later, his cousins lying next to him in the beds and on the floor, whispering and giggling and nudging each other, trying to sleep so Santa would come and trying to stay awake so that the moment might last forever; the scramble the next morning to the living room where toys and packages were crammed under the tree and baggy eyed adults smiled approval. Later, the whole clan would sit on the hard pew in the church while the minister who so often seemed angry and unyielding to Rainwater when he was little told the story again, his voice now soothing and unreproachful. Then they would ride home from church in a small parade of sedans and station wagons, quiet and thoughtful, appreciating Jesus and Santa.

Then Rainwater recalled the Christmas when he had left, when he had tried yet again to recapture those feelings of security and certainty and warmth but had again failed. The small, pale plastic tree in his family's tiny apartment had seemed so empty and the space below it had been even emptier. They had so little to buy presents for the girls, to recapture that feeling he had had as a child himself. Only his best friend Don and his wife and son were supposed to come over that day and Rainwater remembered how desperately lonely he had felt. The aunts and uncles were all old or dead; his mother and father too feeble to travel; cousins all scattered across the country. He had the swing shift at work, so he had not gone to church that day with the family, but had sent them off to church and gotten a ride with Don to work, and then the accident where he had killed his best friend Don. He still saw the image, his pal crushed under the crates, the forklift sitting on top of him. After the accident, Rainwater left the factory and just walked away. He had only wanted to walk and think and decide what to do, but the walking had felt good and he had walked away. And walking away, he had decided, would keep his family safe, safe from knowing his mistakes and safe from what he had done.

Rainwater sat up now and reached into his coat pocket and pulled out a small, thin bottle. He unscrewed the top and sucked a gulp of bitter, oily gin. He grimaced as he licked his lips and leaned back against the flat, hard pillow of the bed. He held the bottle upright next to him. Why had it been so difficult to recapture those feelings when he was grown, to reconstruct the scenes he had remembered so fondly from his childhood? He thought about his daughters and the scenes they must have of Christmas as children. Again, he pictured them at their mother's, laughing and cooking. He tried to imagine her as grey and plump and smiling while the kids piled out of their mini-vans, but he saw a picture of her as small and angry, tired. Her sister who never married, a cold, unyielding woman as he saw her, might be there, too, sharing his family with her sister over the holiday. Rainwater picked up the bottle again and pulled a longer swallow from it. He barely moved his head as he drank. He tried to imagined his grandchildren, if he had any. They might be older now, for all he knew, restless to be moving on, to be free. What pictures his daughters must have. What stories did they not tell?

They had their own lives now, and it hadn't had anything to do with him. They made their own memories too, memories that did not include James Allen Rainwater, happy memories. He had not been tempted to go back and see them because he knew they didn't want to see him. He knew they knew he was a killer, that he was responsible for Don's death. He raised the little bottle of gin and gulped a long swallow, finishing it off. He replaced the top and reached over towards the floor, dropping the bottle the last few inches to keep from having to raise himself up. The bottle landed with a faint echo. He realized he had no way of knowing Sandy's last name now. How would he find her address?

It was starting to get dark outside. Rainwater reached up and flipped the light switch and the room changed. It was almost dark in the room and the window let in a pale blue light from the street lights reflecting off the snow on the rooftops. He could see the snow better now with the light off. He stared out the window. Each flake fell into the mass of flakes that gathered on the rooftop outside and the ledge of the window. He watched the snowflakes wafting without direction except what direction the wind and gravity provided. Down the street, a sign from a liquor store came on and Rainwater watched the patterns of flashing red and green lights reflect off the ceiling. After a while, he took the letter out of his pocket and read it again in the pale light from the window. He held it in his coarse, gnarled hands for several minutes, then crumpled it and threw it toward the sink. He rolled over on his side and tried to sleep.

Sideshow

Worked in a bar once, tending bar. Wasn't much to it. It was a little neighborhood pub with about twenty regulars who came in each day to get a drink and talk to each other and all. There was one guy, was a postman, and he would come in everyday exactly at four-thirty. I'd see him and open a light beer and take it to the end of the bar, take his money and go get another one and take it to him. Before I had his money in the register, he was out the door. Just like clockwork. I don't know. Maybe he wasn't allowed to drink at home.

Part 1

The road fell away from the hill crest and curved out of the trees. As the old man came down the pavement, walking slowly, deliberately towards the small town that had promised itself on a sign a mile back, he couldn't help but see the tent. It was large and conspicuous in front of the discount department store, although what had surely once been bright yellow and green stripes on the tent had faded to an even drabness. When the old man came closer, he saw the battered, hand-lettered sign which billed the attraction as "The Stupendous Traveling Celebrity Circus!" The tent was the first place he came to, and as good a spot to seek a little shelter and food as any, he supposed.

The old man approached the tent flap from the road. A small travel trailer was parked on the far side of the tent, but otherwise, the place looked deserted. When he neared the tent, however, he heard voices. He pulled back the flap and peered in. A man and a woman were inside the tent. The man slumped on a stool, his back to the flap, but he was clearly a large, round man with a very shiny bald head. The tent was warm in the early spring sun. The old man smelled the odor of dogs. The fat man on the stool took a long, slow drink from a plastic cup. The woman was beyond the heavy man, fidgeting with a small round stool covered with sequins. She was short, somewhat squat with red yellow hair that maybe was supposed to be blonde. She rolled the stand across the ground and was clearly quite pigeon toed; she gave the old man the impression of waddling. The two people in the tent must have noticed that a shadow filled the doorway of the tent at the same time and they turned their heads tiredly. The old man stood there, quiet, a bag over one shoulder, a coat in one hand, and a battered rain hat in the other.

"Next show's at three, fella," the fat man sneered.

"Thank you, but I'm not here for the show. I'm looking for work, odd jobs, clean up, what have you. I'll work cheap." He paused to let his offer sink in. He glanced around the tent now and realized they probably had little more than he. It was smaller inside than it had looked from the outside. Two short rows of simple wooden benches took up much of the tent. A tired plywood ring was cracked and needed painting and filled the center of the tent. A few stands, a basket full of sequined pins and balls, and some dogs in a small pen, and the tent seemed surprisingly congested.

"Well, we ain't got nothin' to pay you with, so you'd better move on," growled the fat man with a wave. He turned away from the flap and took another long drink from his cup.

"I don't need much. Some food maybe. A few dollars." The old man's pale blue eyes were sincere, as they had been many times before. He sought out the woman's eyes, caught them, and stared intently at her. She looked back at him for a moment, then set her lips in a thin straight line.

"Hal, we do need things that need to be done." She spoke to the fat man, her voice more resigned than convincing. The old man almost felt sorry for his posturing just listening to her talk. "Seems like Bob's always so busy, and all you do is drown yourself in whiskey and self-pity. We could use some help." She turned now towards the old man. "There isn't much to pay you with, but you can eat and maybe sleep here in the tent tonight if it doesn't get too cold." She spoke in an accent that could have been from Serbia, the Ukraine, or South America, but seemed somehow forced. The man on the stool turned again and looked at the old beggar standing just inside the tent now. He rolled his eyes and lifted the cup to his mouth.

"And you'd better get dressed, Hal. It's almost two." There was a hint of admonishment in her accent.

"Okay, okay, Jan," Hal moaned. "Damn, why do I bother?" He picked up a bottle that had evidently been perched between his feet, rose, and went out the flap. As he passed out the doorway, another man came in, this one thin, dark-haired, with deep wrinkles across his cheeks and forehead. He had a large bag of dog food in one hand and a small bag of groceries in the other.

"Hello. What's this?" He was surprised to see the old man standing in the tent.

"Folks call me Rainwater, sir."

"He needs work, Bob, and food," Jan interrupted. Bob looked suddenly at the small bag of groceries in his hand. "He can have some of mine if we're short." The woman turned to Rainwater. "Can you fix the ring there? We need it for the next show."

"Yes ma'am." Rainwater swung his bag from his shoulder and dropped it and his coat on the bleachers. "Got any tools?"

When the woman had gone to get the tools from the trailer, Bob went over to Rainwater. "Listen, friend. We ain't got any money or food to spare. Here's two dollars; it's all I got, but don't take any food. You fix the ring if you can; I don't want Jan sayin' I chased you off. But you leave after the show, okay?" He was not threatening, and Rainwater knew he was being generous with what he had.

"Yes, sir. I understand."

Jan came back with a hammer and several plastic jars of nails. Rainwater inspected the ring and began sorting through a basket of nails the woman had brought him. Bob took off his jacket and pulled a red coat with long tails along with a black top hat out of a crate next to the dog pen. The coat was getting thread-bare shiny and the hat was tattered in places, but with his black hair and rugged face, he looked a bit like a circus barker. The heavy man, Hal, came in dressed as a clown, complete with a powdered white face, although his head still shone. He had cross covered eyes, a large scarlet bow tie, and a ridiculous, green plaid, three-piece polyester suit, also shiny with age. Jan was using the stool as a desk and started printing cards with a rubber stamp and an old red stamp pad, her back to Hal, who stood massive, but limp, at the edge of the tent. The dogs whined and she stopped pressing the stamp onto the note cards and went over to the little cage, cooing and petting the dogs through the wire top.

Hal sat suddenly on the edge of the ring and grunted, staring at the ground. "We're celebrities, you know," he said more or less to Rainwater. The old man looked up at him and cocked one eyebrow. "Oh, yeah. We're stars. Surely, you've heard of us. I'm Hal Johnston. I'm the clown, as you can see, as well as the strong man, gimmick guy, and I will be the cause of any errors that might befall any of the acts. That fellow there is Robert Wilson, who likes to be called 'Rango' when he's performing. He's our ringmaster, whip snapper, rope twirler, and amazing juggler." Bob looked over at Hal out of the corner of his eye. Rainwater sat still, frozen with the basket in his hands. He wasn't sure what he was supposed to say. "And here," Hal stood now and gestured grandly, "here is the star of our show, my sister, Janet Johnston, also known as Madame Moriot, whose trained dogs, Pookie and Limey, make up Madame Moriot's Curley Currs." The woman managed a small smile for Rainwater, which made him feel released from the conversation. He looked back at the basket and picked out several small nails to drive into the small crack in the plywood. Rainwater could see Bob the ringmaster bustling about the edge of the tent, sorting and resorting the sets of balls and pins. Bob stood back a minute, then disappeared through the tent flap.

The clown walked over to the stool and leaned over it with both hands on the seat. "Dammit, Jan," he said in a slow voice. "I'm tired. I'm really tired." Rainwater focused on the ring he was supposed to fix. He tapped the thin nails into the soft wood. "Why are we still doing this, Jan? Tell me the truth, don't you ever get tired of doing all this? I mean, think about it. We been doin' these same acts twice a day for, well, hell, for years. Now tell me the truth, don't you sometimes feel like just layin' down and sayin', 'I've had it. I give up. I wanna go home.'" Jan idly pet the two little dogs. She did not stand up or turn around. "Dammit, Jan, it just ain't no fun no more, you know?" He released one hand to gesture, but still rested his cumbersome weight on the stool with the other hand. "When we first started, it was a lark, just something for three young people to do to make a little money when there weren't any jobs around. But now, you know now sometimes I think we're trapped in it. Sometimes I think we do it because we can't do nothin' else." Rainwater looked up at the man and then at the woman, but she didn't seem to be paying attention to the big man talking to her back. "Sometimes I feel like takin' that old twenty two of Bob's and putting a hole in my head." Rainwater looked back at the ring quickly. His eyes were wide. He tried to focus on his peripheral vision so he could see them talking, but he didn't want to be seen eavesdropping, although they made no attempt to lower their voices. He tried to busy himself sorting more nails out of the basket. Hal turned around and sat on the stool, flattening the cards that were there, but he didn't seem to care.

"Hal, please don't talk like that," the woman said now without an accent. She did not turn and was still petting the dogs who wagged their tails eagerly. "You know I can't stand it when you talk like that. Bob's happy enough, isn't he? Why is it so bad?" Now she stood and faced Hal. "Why does it have to be so bad?" She wrinkled her brow and held out her hands. She was almost begging. She turned her back to him again and looked at the dogs as they circled in their little pen. "It's not fair for you to talk to me like that, Hal. You can't put everything on me. You want to quit, quit. You want to shoot yourself, go ahead. Shoot yourself. You want to move on, move on, Hal. Just don't talk to me about it. I guess I don't need to know why we do these shows. It's just what we do, okay? It just seemed natural at the time, though, didn't it?"

"Well, maybe then." Hal looked at the ground, but his focus was somewhere else.

"Sure, Hal. It was fun, once, wasn't it? I mean, I was always good with Momma's dogs and you were always such a cut-up. Everyone's always thought you were a hoot, Hal." She turned and looked at him briefly and smiled a wan smile at him, then turned back around to the dogs.

"Yeah, sure, the jolly fat man. That's me." Hal looked very tired, sitting almost motionless on the stool.

"I didn't mean that, Hal." She turned and looked at him evenly.

"I know."

"But you could always make me laugh, Hal." She turned towards the flap.

"You haven't laughed in a long time, Jan. I'm not so funny anymore, am I?" Hal was watching her movements. Rainwater tried to nail softly so he wouldn't disturb their conversation. He wished he'd gone to the department store. "I just wish we could go back to Masonville, Jan. I wish we could just dump this sorry show and go on back and start over again."

She turned to him again and seemed to look hard at his shiny forehead. "Just what is it you want me to do, Hal? I can't live my life and yours, too, you know."

"I'm sorry, Jan. I guess it's that promise we made, you know."

"Jesus, Hal, we were just kids. You're not bound by that anymore." She threw her hands up in a small gesture of disbelief.

"Bob thinks we are, Jan."

"Oh, forget that, Hal. Bob will be fine. For God's sake, if you're not happy here, move on."

"But what about you, Jan? What do you want? Hell, we can't keep on doing this forever, you know. You know, Bob worries about you the most." Rainwater heard Jan sigh deeply.

"Me? Aren't we all in this together?" She held her hands out again. "What's he think, I can't do anything else but play with these dogs?"

"Well, you know that Bob still thinks that maybe you and he will . . ."

"Oh, for Christ's sake!" She yelled and spun now and walked back to the dog cage. "Not again. Jesus! Haven't we been here enough?" She sighed again as Bob came back into the tent carrying a coil of rope. Hal and Jan looked quickly at each other and fell silent. Hal stood up and began stuffing one of the cards Jan had printed and three balloons into small plastic bags. Bob dropped the rope onto a basket already full of small balls and began sealing the bags Hal had filled with an iron.

"These here are Balloon Dog Kits." Hal called too loudly to Rainwater. "They sell for fifty cents each which usually adds about two dollars a show to our piddly take at the gate." Rainwater nodded an acknowledgement without looking up. Jan stood still, her arms at her side limply and looked at Hal. She shook her head and walked through the flap. The tent was quiet, except for Rainwater's hammering, for several minutes while the men busied themselves with small chores. A few minutes later, Jan came back into the tent. She had changed into a drummer boy outfit and now she walked over to the dog pen and began removing waste from it. She grimaced as she leaned over the pen, scooping. Rainwater pounded on the ring, which was clearly not all that badly damaged. What's more, it looked like it had been broken for a long time.

"It's almost time, Jan," Bob said evenly as he gathered up the packages with the balloons and cards in them and put them into the concession rack, which appeared to be a converted chip rack partially filled with these balloon kits, some dusty American flags, and an assortment of old decals and bumper stickers.

"Right, Bob." She stepped through the tent opening, holding the scoop away from her.

"God, another day, another show. This is the life, ain't it, Bob? Show biz!" Hal went over and sat on the bleachers.

"Aw, shut up, Hal. Come over here and help me move this rack back a little."

"Why? It's the same place it's been for years, Bob. What difference does it make where it is? Damn, don't you ever get tired of doing this, Mr. Rango?" Hal rocked his head side to side a little at the end and said the name with a sing-song tone.

Rainwater looked up, but Bob seemed to ignore the sarcasm and started scooting the rack by himself. "What's the big deal, Hal? We do it. We get away with it. Sometimes we even enjoy it, don't we? Remember that guy with the beard that time who kept snorting at the lady next to him? I thought she was going to kill him." He chuckled a little.

"My God, Bob, that was five years ago. I don't get it. How long can you go on nothing more than memories? What is it you get from all this, huh? So the show's got to go on, eh? Well, I don't need it, Bob." Hal shook his head slowly. "I just can't do it anymore, Bob. Dammit, I quit." His voice sounded firm. Rainwater turned and looked at the two men. Hal stood now, a serious frown mocking his clown face and garb. The light from the doorway reflected off his shiny head.

"Jan's not quitting and I'm not quitting. Come on, Hal, it's time to get ready." Bob didn't even look at Hal who rolled his eyes, then looked at Rainwater and shrugged. Bob looked over at Rainwater. "If you want to stay for the show, that's fine. We'll start in about ten minutes." Hal looked at Rainwater now with a vague expression of despair. Rainwater stopped nailing and looked over at the man. He was not that old, perhaps early thirties, Rainwater figured, although the clown garb made that guesswork. He looked familiar, like Rainwater himself had looked perhaps once, although there were no physical similarities. Maybe it was the posture, the facial expression, the eyes; he looked like defeat. That was it. His eyes. The clown gazed towards Rainwater for a long moment, then shook his head, looked at the ground, and walked through the flap after Bob, leaving Rainwater alone in the tent. Vague scratchy circus music started playing over some tiny speakers tucked behind the dog pen.

Part 2

Three children with their mother came into the tent and Rainwater picked up his coat and hat and slid them under a bench along with the hammer and baskets of rusty nails. He sat at the end and waited for the show. Other parents and children walked eagerly into the tent.

The tent was nearly filled, due greatly to the smallness of it, when Hal bounced through the flap and out into the ring with a joyous smile on his mouth, although his eyes seemed focused on some point distant. The same vague circus music played as he pranced impishly, waving limp wrist at the children on all sides, over and again. There was little response, perhaps a wave or two, but the children seemed to be waiting for something to happen, although some parents smiled, no doubt in anticipation of the fun their children would soon be having. Finally, he stopped prancing and squeaked, "I know." He walked over to the edge of the plywood ring Rainwater had repaired and fairly yelled, "Howdy!" He put his hand up to his ear to evoke a response from the children, but there was none. Perhaps the children wanted something more. He went over to the other side of the ring. "Howdy!" Again he listened for a response.

A couple of children at one end of the bench murmured, "Howdy." Rainwater said a small "Howdy" as well, although he felt awkward. Still, it seemed the polite thing to do.

"I can't hear you," the clown squeaked. "Howdy!" Hand up to his ear.

"Howdy," three children on the other side said.

"How about over here?" He walked back across the tent. "Howdy!"

"Howdy!" Six or seven responded this time.

"How about over here again?" He paced back and forth. "Howdy!" Rainwater noticed a sweat break out on Hal's shiny head.

"Howdy!" The ice was breaking.

"I know. I bet you'd like a balloon over here."

"Yeah!" The children were beginning to squeal as Rainwater looked on with doubt. Was this the show? Hal blew up a balloon and snapped it into the crowd. A slight scramble followed as the children dashed for the prize.

"How about over here?"

"Yeah!" It was the tinny sound of excited children. He blew up another balloon and snapped it into the crowd.

"Another one over here?"

"Yeah," came the screaming whines.

Another was snapped into the crowd. The clown blew up another balloon until it popped, then pretended to cry over it and placed it carefully on a stand used in the dog act. The tent filled a little more now, to maybe twenty people.

"I bet you'd like a dog over here," he yelled, twisting two balloons together. It was clearly a lead-in to the gimmick.

"Yeah!"

"How about over here?" He twisted two balloons.

"Yeah!"

The bribing went on for several more minutes until Bob stepped through the flap, blew his whistle and spoke over the fuzzy sound system, although it was hardly necessary. "Thank you. Thank you. How about a big hand for our favorite clown, Professor Inkwell?" An excited applause of small hands arose, but Rainwater could see the parents were getting doubtful. He himself wondered about it. It did not seem like an act exactly, but the children seemed to like it, so they could all go along. "After the show, Professor Inkwell will be selling kits with everything necessary to make your own balloon dogs. The Professor will return after the show with the entire cast to meet and talk to all the kids, young and old, who wish to meet the players." Another shriek of his whistle came as he put down the microphone and picked up three balls from the basket. The juggling act was rather brief, using different articles in the same tricks. He bounced the balls off his head, threw them up two at a time, did similar feats with plastic rings, which he dropped once, and did the tricks again using plastic, sequin covered pins, ending in a twisting hop that seemed out of place, but did, at least, seem to end the act. He stood with his arms out stretched and bowed. There was another, less enthusiastic round of applause.

"Thank you. Thank you," he panted too heavily for what he had done. Rainwater tried to remove the scowl of disbelief from his forehead. He had certainly seen better juggling. Bob caught his breath quickly and removed his top hat. "Of course, no circus is complete without a strong man, and we have here with us today the strongest man in the world, our own Professor Inkwell." He raised his arm and waved toward the opening in the tent. There was a hush that sounded like disappointment; they were already using the same players. Hal shuffled in, with rope trailing from each hand.

"I'm the strongest man there is," he gloated childishly. "I'm the strongest man in the whole world." He turned for the audience.

"What are you doing with those ropes, Professor?"

"Why, Mr. Rango," Hal said too happily. Rainwater heard that same sing-song in his voice, but perhaps no one else did. "I'm gonna have a tug of war with this here little girl to prove I'm the strongest man in the world." He pulled a frightened eight-year-old out of the crowd. He gave her one end of one of the ropes.

"Wait a minute! That's no contest for the strongest man in the world. Here, you help. And you." Bob pointed. "And you, you, and you, and how about a couple more over here." Children were waving their arms to be chosen. Some were climbing over the crowded audience to stand in the middle of the ring where the clown was standing, looking very tired. "Okay, one more here. How about you." The children not chosen lowered their hands, their faces portraits of a tiny disappointment. "Now some of you take this rope," Bob pushed the children where he wanted them to be, "and some of you take this one. Now let's see if we can make two Professor Inkwells." The corny name was beginning to sound old even to Rainwater. The children lined up on each side of the clown, his arms open between them. The clown pretended to dig in his heels. "Okay, ready? Pull!" Bob dropped his hand as if starting a race. The rope pulled taut and obviously went through the clown's coat so that the children were pulling against each other. Hal slipped off the coat and feigned a hearty but silent laugh.

"Boy, never saw that coming," someone behind Rainwater said. The crowd tittered over the remark.

"Oh, you tricked us, Professor!" Bob gave a forced chuckle. "How about a hand for Professor Inkwell, the world's strongest man?"

There was only scattered response. Rainwater looked around the tent. The corny, amateurish acts, the increasing heat and the overpowering ammoniacal smell of the dogs had already driven away several people. But it probably didn't matter, since they had already paid. Bob went into his lasso routine, ending with the dubious feat of twirling a small lasso in each hand and another from a pole attached to his rear. He ended with a twisting hop as incongruous as the first. There was scattered response as he stood there with hands outstretched, panting. Professor Inkwell was called out yet again to make more balloon dogs. Janet came in as Madame Moriot, taking the dogs through their routine. They walked atop balls, jumped through hoops, and danced. It was all done to Parisian Can Can music which played on the fuzzy sound system.

Bob ring mastered through the act, noting the difficulty of each trick. The show ended with Bob cracking a whip at a target held by a child who looked like she was terrified, and twirling a fifty-foot rope, ending each with a twisting hop and a shriek of his whistle. The now sparse audience, numbering maybe ten, was reminded of the balloon kits, thanked, invited ringside for autographs, and released. Rainwater still sat on the bleacher. He could not decide whether to go over to his three employers because the show had been so bad, to him, he could not bring himself to compliment them. The audience filed out murmuring.

The show had lasted almost exactly twenty minutes. Rainwater supposed it always did. He watched his three employers sell four of the balloon kits and saw a man in an NRA cap steal a six-inch American flag. Bob gave his scratchy autograph to three children who seemed something less than overwhelmed. The last child left with her mother who looked back at Jan with a pitying glance and a shake of her head.

Hal unbuttoned his coat and wiped his brow with a handkerchief, smearing the white, caked powder. Rainwater reached to pick up the hammer to return it and leave, as he had promised. It had been kicked under the bottom of the bench and he stooped to pick it up. Jan said something about getting a bowl to feed the dogs and walked through the flap.

Hal sat heavily on the stool. "Gawd, Bob, what a life. Let's go get a bottle of gin and drink to the good life, huh? Whatta ya say?" He rubbed his shiny head.

"Yeah, why not," Bob said in a voice almost as tired as Hal's. His body looked tired as well. "I've got a bottle of scotch, Hal, that's almost full. It's out in the trailer. I'll go get it." He was evidently glad the show was over too. He slipped through the door flap.

"Oh, well, uh, don't bother, Bob," Hal called after him in a sheepish voice. "It's, uh, it's gone. I already drank it." Bob came back in slowly and looked sourly at Hal. "Well, you want me to perform, and you won't let me quit; I just needed a little pick me up before the show." Hal shrugged apologetically. He seemed uneasy under Bob's stare.

"Goddammit, Hal, you stay out of my stuff. I've been saving that scotch for two weeks and now you've gone and drunk it up. What the hell gives you the right to take my stuff, huh?" The two men stared at each other, Bob glaring in anger, Hal frowning defensively. They seemed to take no notice of Rainwater who stooped over the bench, reaching for the hammer, wishing to leave as soon as possible. Bob began pacing and wringing his hands. His anger grew obvious, as if there were something much more going on. "You know, this isn't the first time you've done this, either, now that I think about it. Just because you're a complainer doesn't give you the right to steal my stuff, Hal." He shook his finger at him.

Hal looked up, scowling. "Now wait a minute. I didn't steal nothin'. What's mine is yours and what's yours is mine. That was one of those rules we made at the very beginning. It's always been like that since we started this sorry little show, and you know it. And you know what? Maybe I am a complainer, but the fact is, I'm right about this stupid show. And what's more, I've had it. I've had it up to here." He held his hand up to his cross-covered eyes. Hal was yelling now and Bob was frowning down at him. Rainwater had retrieved the hammer, but now he wondered what to do with it. The two men were getting very agitated and all Rainwater wanted to do was leave. Jan walked into the tent, a bowl of dog food in one hand, a bowl of water in the other. The two men were embarrassed by her entrance, creating an awkward silence. Hal and Bob were looking intensely at each other and Janet looked quizzically at the two of them. Finally, Bob's pent up anger could stand it no longer.

"Well, maybe this show wouldn't be so bad if you'd try a little bit," he yelled at Hal. "You haven't given a damn about anything for a long time now, Hal. All you ever think about is yourself and that's it. You're always feeling sorry for yourself and bitchin' and moanin'. Ah, hell, you're nothing but a loser, Hal, and I don't know why I ever let you stay on here in the first place." He waved Hal away and turned towards the tent opening.

If he had had tried to hurt Hal, it was clear he had not. Hal stood now and reached into the basket that held the balls, pins, and hoops and retrieved the plastic cup he had been drinking out before from where it had been tossed into the basket. He sneered and held up the cup. "Well, here's to losers, Rango." His voice was wet with sarcasm. Jan stood back next to the dogs, staring at the two men. She looked bewildered and sought out Rainwater's eyes with a silent plea for him to do something. There was a moment of silence as Hal's barb sank in and Bob evidently thought of his defense. In the brief pause, Rainwater placed the hammer on the ring, picked up his coat and bag, and headed for the door. Jan called to him, as if his leaving would be disastrous.

"Wait, Mister. You haven't been paid."

"The name's Rainwater, ma'am, and yes ma'am, I've been paid and I'm leaving as I promised." He looked at Bob, who glanced at Rainwater then resumed his stare at Hal. Rainwater stepped through the flap. Jan followed Rainwater, flipping the tent flap open as she did. Rainwater heard the plastic cup inside fall onto the pavement that made the floor of the tent.

Bob's voice was a low growl. "You worthless ass. You think you're funny, don't you? Well, I'll tell you what, funny man; these dogs are smarter than you, Hal, and they're better actors, too. I should have fired you years ago." Rainwater paused outside the tent to adjust the pack on his shoulder. He looked back at the two men squared off before each other in the tent.

"Hey, fine by me, Mr. Rango," Hal mocked. "I've been hoping to leave this three-dog show for a long time now."

"What do you mean by that?" Bob's voice was quick and loud now. "You got something to say, say it, dammit."

"Aw hell, you know what I mean, Bob. You know damn well what I mean. Why don't you open your eyes, stupid? You think I'm a loser, well, at least I don't lose out to Fido." Bob was curiously quiet. Hal pressed his advantage. "You're a fool, Bob. And I'm a damn fool for sitting around here all this time so I could watch you being a fool. You want a good act? Look at your life. Aw, shit. What's the use? You ain't got the sense to see the nose on your own God-damn face." As Rainwater turned and stepped on the sidewalk outside the tent, he heard a grunting curse and a sickening thud as Bob smashed his fist into the side of Hal's shiny head, knocking him to the pavement. Jan tugged on Rainwater's sleeve. Rainwater could hear Hal inside cursing and spitting blood on the pavement.

"Please don't leave, please," Jan begged. "I've never seen them like this before. I don't know what it's all about. They're . . .they've gone crazy." Her eyes were wide with fear. "I mean, we argue sometimes, but nothing like this."

"It's been coming, I'd say." Rainwater turned to face her. Inside, the two men were yelling again.

"That does it. I'm gone. I'm out of here. You're out of your fuckin' head, Bob. You're damned crazy is what. You're absolutely, fuckin' crazy."

"Oh, no you don't. We agreed to stay together until we all agreed to quit. I ain't quitting and neither are you."

"After that?" Hal laughed in disgust. "You try and stop me, ass-hole." Bob gagged as Hal drove his fist into his stomach.

Now there were thuds and crashes and curses as the two men thrashed at each other. They screamed, half crying, and swung wildly. Rainwater and Jan stood watching the tent, almost expecting it to fall as the men fell into the side of it.

"Please stop them. They'll kill each other. I just don't know what they want anymore." She turned and faced Rainwater. Her eyes filled with tears. "Seems like all they ever do is put me in the middle of some argument or another." She was talking quickly now, with no accent. "Hal's so unhappy and Bob seems so tired all the time." She ran her hand through her hair. "God, sometimes I do wonder why we keep on doing this thing. But now this." She turned and looked at the tent again where the men were crashing over the display and props as they wrestled and swung savagely. "We can't just stand here." She looked back at Rainwater. "Please help me. Please."

"No, ma'am. I don't think I can help you. Besides, I don't think you need my help." She looked at him, her face looking bewildered and a little angered by what must have seemed his riddle of an answer. Rainwater looked down into her face. He reached out and put his free hand on her shoulder. "They're fighting over you, I'd say. Over what you want and more, maybe. But I don't know what more. I don't think they'll kill each other. But I do think there's evidently something you're going to have to decide. And soon." Rainwater dropped his hand and turned away from Jan. He walked towards the department store behind the curious crowd that had gathered outside the tent. Rainwater turned when he reached the edge of the pavement. Janet was still watching him. She was crying more heavily now. The crowd gawked at her red eyes. Some women holding children tittered as she passed and Rainwater heard one say loudly as she turned to go past them, "Sounds like them 'Curley Currs' is actin' up, Madame Mory-ott," and the crowd laughed and some pointed at her as she worked her way towards the tent. Janet looked confused in the growing crowd outside the tent where the two men were still thrashing at each other. Her eyes were wide, unfocused. Her face was drawn and pale. A deep, heavy frown dominated her face and she blinked away tears. Hal and Bob fell into the side of the tent, pushing it out and ripping it some. A cheer went up from the crowd. "You oughta sell tickets to this," one young man in a red cap yelled at Janet as she turned and tried to change directions in the crowd. She didn't seem to be sure where she wanted to go. Rainwater could hear various comments about the quality of the acts being yelled at her, and some men were laughing heartily over a comment about finally getting their money's worth. The crowd was buzzing now, and some snickered and laughed out loud just to see her. Janet turned in the crowd as if she were lost, then she waddled suddenly away from the crowd and behind the tent towards the small trailer. Rainwater walked away, shaking his head. He stood in front of the window of the store and looked absent mindedly at his tired reflection in the window. A pistol shot rang out and then another. He turned to the tent. The crowd was silent now and drifted back defensively. Rainwater dropped his bag and ran back to the flap on the tent which had been partially ripped in the fight. Inside, it was quiet. Rainwater pushed through the crowd and approached the tent cautiously.

"Hello? Um, Jan?"

"Yeah." Her voice was slow and even. Rainwater looked in and she looked up at him, the pistol still in her hand. Hal was lying on the overturned souvenir rack, dabbing his cuts with a handkerchief. Bob was leaning over the dog cage, staring down wide-eyed. Limey and Pookie lay still in a pool of blood, their eyes open.

Funspot

I've walked a thousand miles, I guess. All over this country. Every place you go, big city, little country town, or just someplace in the middle of nowhere, there's folks looking out for each other. Guess it feeds us somewhere deep down to reach out and give someone a hand. Course, I've seen plenty of the other kind of folks too. Kids who will throw things at you just to be mean. People yell out their car windows, telling me I ain't worth living, that I ought to do the world a favor and just die already. You believe that? And mind you, these are folks I never asked a thing from. Just mean. But I can take it. Sometimes, I think I deserve it. Afterall, I don't add anything to society, I don't guess. Except maybe I give folks someone they can look down on and hate. Seems like a lot of people need someone to look down on.

The ocean let out a deep throated hiss as it swallowed the beach, gave it up, and swallowed it again, taking a little less with each wave. Sand pipers hopped about the receding water, pecking at tiny shells that rolled back to the ocean and then washed back up again only to roll back down into the surf. The sun and the sand were warm and yellow. A slight breeze blew the salt air toward the slow rising hills in the distance. Rainwater walked slowly, heavily, along the shore, his bare feet sinking comfortably into the wet sand. His pack was slung over his shoulder. His back hurt. Some distance ahead of him, he saw a black man back away from the water, his hand turning a reel handle quickly, his fishing rod bent toward the water. Bluefish maybe, thought Rainwater. He slipped a little on a drying jelly fish buried in the sand as he watched the man reel in his line. The farther Rainwater walked, the more the beach grew uneven with clumps of grass springing up along the dunes and remnants of old picket fences beaten down by the tides.

As he strolled along the edge of the waves, he watched the sand and the way his feet made shallow depressions in the water-hardened sand, the foot impressions filling quickly with foamy water. Gulls circled, crying. When he looked up, he saw a fence with a large sign, which read: Government Property. And below that, in red letters: Keep out. He turned around and walked along the waves now so that they could lick at his feet and splash his toes with the cool, frothy water. Walking towards the clump of high-rise hotels that was farther down the beach, he began to tire and his steps slowed. At the edge of the boardwalk, an amusement park, closed for the season, absorbed the pale but warming sun, a limp sign wagging slowly in the wind proclaiming it a "Funspot." The rides were still. Nobody comes in January because it was too far up the coast, thought Rainwater, and what a pity that was. That was when the beach was really at its best; the sea full of both rage and peace, the grey storms powerful and majestic.

A brown and white dog slept under a bench beside the bumper cars which were all bunched haphazardly in a corner. He whined as the old man approached. The dog lifted his head and, crouching, wagged his tail. Then he inched toward Rainwater, his eyes looking up, his tail tucked but wagging. Rainwater looked into his bag which he had swung onto the bench and pulled out half a sandwich wrapped in a napkin.

"When's the last time you ate, fellow?" The dog looked up, standing taller now. "Here you go, probably not too good any more anyway. I imagine it's pretty soggy by now." He tossed the sandwich before the dog which ate it hungrily in a gulp. The dog looked up at him again and wagged his tail. "Sorry, boy, that's all I got." Rainwater shrugged.

"H'yere, Zack, h'yere boy." The black man was walking up the beach with his rod in one hand and a bucket in the other. The dog loped off toward him. "H'yere, Zack!" The fisherman called again as the dog came up to him. Rainwater laughed as he watched the dog run towards his master.

"You old faker," he called after the dog, but his voice was drowned by the surf. The dog and his master walked off along the beach. Rainwater stood up and arched his back, stretching his arms up. He stood with his feet apart, his hands on his hips for a moment, looking at the quiet town that stretched up the beach from the edge of the ocean. "Probably half a million come springtime," he said aloud, his voice muffled by the steady breeze and waves. He dusted the sand off his feet, pulled on some stiff socks, and put on his heavy shoes. Picking up his bag, he walked off across the board walk to the row of stores beyond the big hotels. Some of the hotels were closed. Most of the stores were closed.

He walked down a side street towards a small delicatessen that appeared to be open, but he really couldn't tell from the outside. When he went in, he was surprised to find maybe twenty people sitting at the tables, talking quietly and familiarly. A long-haired guitarist was playing and singing, although not very well, in the corner. Three waitresses with red bandannas on their heads were scurrying from table to table. Rainwater avoided the tables, going instead to the side which had a counter top and a meat case. A young man in a suit came over, wiping his hands on a towel. Behind him, a clerk was busy slicing meat on a whining machine.

"Help you?"

"Is the boss here? I mean, the manager or someone?"

"That's me. What can I do for you?" He stood with his hands on his hips now.

"I'm real hungry and looking for work. I'll work hard for a few dollars." Rainwater looked for the man's eyes, but he had turned away.

"Sorry, no jobs today. Check down at the warehouse." He started to walk away.

"Please," Rainwater begged. "I'll do most anything. I'm real hungry."

The young man turned around and looked hard at the dilapidated man with the long beard. "I said I don't have anything. Move on before I call the cops." His voice rose a bit and the customers at the nearest table looked up curiously. The manager set his mouth firmly.

"I don't care what kind of work it is. I'll do any kind of job you want." Now Rainwater's eyes met the young man's and he took a posture of earnest need.

Rainwater watched as the man looked him over and saw him glance at the table that had looked up. Rainwater imagined his own appearance to the store manager, with his long white hair and scruffy grey beard. He imagined he might look like Moses might have looked. "Well, I've got some cleaning that needs doing in the back. It's pretty nasty," the man said as if to discourage Rainwater, "but if you want to work, I'll pay you five dollars an hour, cash." He said the last part more softly, as if it were a secret.

"I'd be glad to have it." Rainwater picked up his bag to walk behind the meat counter. Five dollars an hour was precious little, but if he would pay cash, it all worked out. And it wasn't as if he had options.

"No, come around to the back door." The young man had his hands up. "I'll show you what needs to be done."

Rainwater turned and walked out the door, found the alley, and went to the back door. The young man was standing, waiting.

"Look, this dumpster is so nasty it's stinking up the whole street. I can't even open the back door without three people inside fainting." He laughed at his joke. When Rainwater only stood and looked at him, he continued with a frown. "They just emptied it a while ago so now's as good as time as any. Here's a hose; there's the faucet." He pointed to the wall. "Just inside here is a bucket, brush, and some disinfectant cleaner. See how fast you can clean it. I'll come back and check on you in a little while." He scowled again, dropped the hose on the ground and turned inside the wide double doors of the delicatessen.

Rainwater swung his bag inside the door, out of the way, and arched his back. The dumpster smelled horrible of spoiled meat and fish. He shook his head, his long, dirty curls dancing about his ears, and picked up the hose. He connected it to the faucet, turned on the water and began spraying down the dumpster. The water made it smell worse. He gagged. Behind him, he heard dishes clinking.

"Good Lord, what an odor," a black woman's voice said. "Whew!" Rainwater turned to see a young black woman, tall, pretty, with a red bandanna on her head, washing dishes in a big double sink just inside the doors.

"Sorry about that. But I'll have it smelling like a rose garden before it's over." He turned and hosed the inside of the dumpster. A brown, foamy fluid ran from the drains at the bottom to the middle of the alley and toward the street. He turned the hose onto the outside of the metal box. "You'll think it was new when I get done."

"Ha. I doubt that," the young woman snorted. "That trash heap ain't been cleaned since I come here, and that's been over a year now." She shook her head, picked up a plate and rubbed a cloth over it. "Glad he found someone to clean it, or I'd've had to do it sooner or later, I bet." She laughed, but it was not a happy laugh. Rainwater was filling the bucket with water and a heavy dose of cleaning fluid. The woman started singing a muted melody as she stood by the sink spraying dishes. I'll start on the outside, Rainwater thought, but, God, how this dumpster stinks. "What he payin' you to get all nasty like that?" the woman asked.

"Five dollars an hour." Rainwater slopped the wet brush on the side of the dumpster. He nearly gagged again.

"Five dollars? Ain't enough. Five dollars." She said softly. "Oh, Lord knows it ain't enough. Course, he never pay enough," she said more loudly. The dishes rattled and Rainwater could hear the clang of pots being dropped into the sink. "I been here over a year, and I ain't had one raise. You believe that?" She was washing a pan and it clanged on the side of the sink. "What you think 'bout a man like that, mister?"

"I don't know, ma'am." Rainwater was scrubbing the metal side, the pine odor of the disinfectant mingling with the stench of the garbage.

"Ma'am? You talkin' to me?" The woman laughed another not-happy laugh. She stacked dishes in a tall single stack and carried them out of sight somewhere inside. She came back with another big tray of dishes. She started singing the same subdued song again. She had a pretty voice, but Rainwater couldn't hear the melody. He looked over at the dishwasher and saw her move her arms in big circles as she scrubbed a platter. She worked hard, first on dishes, then more pots and pans, then dinnerware. Rainwater turned back to the dirty dumpster.

"You ever ask him about it?" Rainwater called without looking.

"Ask who about what?" The woman clanked the dishes noisily behind him.

"Ask your boss about a raise?" He hosed the side of the dumpster and sloshed more disinfectant on the metal. He turned to the door to avoid the reeking garbage.

"Oh yeah." She placed the rack of dishes on a roller belt and pushed it toward the kitchen. "I ask him alright." She glanced out at Rainwater as she crossed the small washing area. "But you know what he says? He say business is off and he might hafta cut back my hours as it is. Oh, Lord. That is bad news. I can't afford that. No sir." She pulled another rack to the edge of the sink. "Mm mm. No sir. Can't afford that," she trailed off as she scoured the dishes in the sink.

Rainwater was getting wet with the soapy water. One side of the outside was nearing completion. He stood up and leaned against the doorway to catch his breath. He looked down the alley towards the street that ran beside the beach.

He could just make out the tops of a few dunes beyond the amusement park in the slowly fading light. He dug his knuckle into the small of his back to loosen the knot that was building there. "Why don't you quit?" he asked blithely. A slow line of pelicans passed the opening of the alley.

The dishwasher laughed a quick snort of disbelief. "Nah, don't suppose my baby'd like that none, or the bill collectors neither." She laughed again and fell back into her song, only louder now, and Rainwater recognized the faint melody of "He Lifted Me." He walked over to the dumpster and started scrubbing another side of the dumpster. The woman behind him grew suddenly quiet.

"How's it coming?" The young man's brassy voice startled Rainwater.

"Okay, I guess. Sure is dirty though." He did not look up, but kept scrubbing on the flat, green surface.

"See if you can't hurry it up. We're gonna need to use that dumpster before long." His voice was flat, the words quick and clipped.

"Yes sir," Rainwater said quietly. His legs were beginning to ache. He could feel the muscles in his calves beginning to tighten in the cooling air. He finished scouring the side and looked up, but the young man was gone.

"So, what? You a drifter or something?" The dishwasher asked when he looked up.

"Yeah, I guess. Just comin' through on my way down south." The cleaning was going faster now but his back was also hurting more. "I'm thinking about settling down in Florida when I get down there. Too cold up here for an old man like me."

"Florida. Mm mm. That'd sure be nice. I sure do like Florida." She pushed a tray of dishes down the conveyer that ran next to the sink and into the kitchen. "Yes sir, I sure do like Florida." The young woman disappeared around the edge of the doorway for a moment, then returned with another large rack of dishes. "Mm mm, I like just the idea of Florida. All that sunshine and oranges and it always stays warm down there. Not like up here where we get all this nasty old cold rain all winter." She arranged the dishes on the tray and hosed them with a large sprayer.

Rainwater scrubbed on the third side of the dumpster. The water chilled his hands while he scrubbed, but, although the work made him feel sick to his stomach, he found he took a certain pride in seeing the green paint on the metal come clean. He stood up now and stretched his back. His knees felt stiff. The dishwasher was humming a different tune now, but Rainwater didn't know what this new tune was. "Well, the way I see it," he said, "you can pretty much go where you like. It's all a matter of making choices and living with the results."

The woman turned to him and put her wet hands on her hips. "Oh, sure. We can all do what we want to. Humph," she waved him away. "Well, that may be alright for you, Mister Drifter. But that ain't the way it is. I can't go where I like."

"Sure you can. You just don't want to. You can do whatever you want, but you just have to be willing to live with the consequences. And sometimes, that's worse than having no choice at all." He picked up the hose and wet the last side of the dumpster. He dropped the hose and splashed cleanser on the metal and started scrubbing again. "Consequences. Yeah those can be tough."

"Well, I got a baby to feed and I got my mamma to take care of, and that means I can't go anywhere. I got no choice. No sir, I got no choice. My life is set the way it is and I got to work here for pennies and I got to hope for a better day. Oh

Lord, I pray every night for a better day." She turned again and began singing a song that Rainwater remembered from his youth when he had gone to church with his parents, "Some Glad Morning." He listened to her singing while he scrubbed. She stopped singing and Rainwater looked up to see where she had gone. She was still washing the dishes with her back to him.

The owner of the deli was standing in the doorway, scribbling on a pad. He looked over at Rainwater who was wet with water and cleanser and perspiration. "That dumpster's looking some better," he nodded. "You get the insides yet?"

"No, not yet," Rainwater panted.

"Well, you'd better get on it. It'll be getting dark before long and you won't be able to see in." The owner looked back at his pad, turned, and walked back inside. The dishwasher began singing again. Rainwater hosed the inside of the dumpster. He listened to the woman singing "This Little Light of Mine." Reaching through the doorway of the dumpster, he scrubbed as far as he could reach without actually having to climb into the dumpster, although at some point he knew he would have to get inside to finish the cleaning.

"You ain't really gonna clean all of that nasty old thing, are you?" The dishwasher was standing in the doorway with her hands on her hips watching him stretch through the opening of the dumpster. "Why, I think they call that cruel an' unusual punishment." She shook her head. "For five dollars an hour? Oh yeah. You got choices. Yeah, you got lots of choices."

Rainwater turned and looked at her. "Yeah, my choices are limited by the consequences of my choices. I guess that's true."

"Yeah, I guess it is. So, you gonna choose to climb into that nasty box?"

"Yeah, I guess I'll have to finish it, or else he might not pay me. I didn't say the consequences were all good. No, ma'am. I've had plenty of bad consequences. And I've made lots of bad choices. Some are the worst choices. Seems like some you just can't outrun." Rainwater trailed off as he spoke. He put one foot on the edge of the dumpster door and reached up for the sides. He pulled himself up onto the edge and teetered there for a moment before hopping in with a squat and a jump. He landed with a splash of milky green water and suppressed an urge to retch.

"Ooh wee!" the woman called, squinching up her nose. Rainwater looked down at his boots then over at the woman with a helpless shrug.

"Could you hand me the bucket there and the hose?" He pointed to the items just outside the bin.

She walked over and handed the bucket to Rainwater. "If you can go anywhere you want, why'd you go in there?"

Rainwater scrubbed the walls. His back was complaining painfully to him. "I was hungry."

The dishwasher turned and walked back into the kitchen. "I guess that's one of them consequences you was talkin' about, huh?" she called out the door as she pulled a rack of dishes over to the sink.

"Yeah, I guess it is." Rainwater grabbed the bottle of disinfectant he had placed on top of the dumpster and splashed healthy streams of cleanser on the sides of the filthy bin.

"Well, I don't think I care for those consequences. No sir, I don't think I care for them one bit." She clattered the dishes.

Rainwater looked up at her. He could just see her back through the opening in the garbage bin. "Well, you wouldn't have to make all the same decisions I did to make changes. I mean, you could go to Florida if you wanted to and get a different job and take your baby and your mother, too, if you wanted to." He shrugged and returned to his scrubbing, his back to the woman.

"Oh, yeah?" The woman came to the doorway and looked out at Rainwater. "Now who you think is gonna hire a black high school drop out with no experience an' no education? An' where we gonna live while I'm out there not gettin' a job? Huh? No, I'm here, alright. I guess I'm bound to stay here. Some choices ain't no choices. My little girl ain't eating out of no garbage bin, and my momma ain't gonna sleep on a grate. I got a place to sleep an' food on the table. Mr. Shires don't pay too much, but he won't let me go. 'Sides, he knows I gotta work to pay the rent on that 'partment o' his I got."

"He rents you a place?"

"Well, yeah, kinda. He takes the rent outa my pay, you know, what I can afford." She returned to her station in front of the sink. She started singing again, but Rainwater couldn't hear the song from inside the dumpster where he was. It was beginning to get darker now.

The woman stopped singing and Rainwater looked up. He could just see the edge of her dress. "Well, at the very least," he called, "you oughta tell your boss that you need more money. You could tell him you might quit even if you didn't intend to." He saw her start visibly.

"Oh, no sir, Mister Drifter. I ain't tell him nothin' of the sort. I'm just mighty glad to have a job an' I don't plan to tell Mister Shires nothin' 'bout quittin' nor anything else for that matter." Rainwater looked through the dumpster door. She was stacking dishes quickly and sliding trays as fast as she could.

"Well, seems to me you oughta do something, Miss. You should get enough money to live off of, anyway. It's just not right, you know?"

The young man in the suit stuck his face suddenly in the doorway of the bin and Rainwater jumped. "Now see here!" he barked. "Just what the hell are you trying to pull here, anyhow?"

Rainwater stood suddenly and his back caught him short of breath. How stupid, he realized. The woman wasn't alone; he hadn't been paying attention. "Oh, well, I didn't mean . . ."

"I know what you didn't mean. You didn't mean for me to hear you trying to cause a bunch of mischief. What do you know about salaries and what's right, anyway?" The owner of the deli stood in the alley, his clip board under his arm, yelling into the trash bin. "Now I want you out of here and I want you out of here now!" He shook his finger at Rainwater. "Or else I'm calling the cops," he added. "We've got vagrancy laws, you know." Rainwater pulled himself out of the nearly clean dumpster with some obvious pain. He landed stiffly on the ground and his back crimped. He arched his back and dug his knuckle between his vertebra. His knees were stiff and achy. His calves felt knotted.

"You owe me ten dollars for my work." Rainwater stood limply before the man. Rainwater was wet to his waist and his shoes were covered with grime and grease.

"I don't owe you a damn thing, you worthless piece of shit. Now you get the hell out of here and consider yourself lucky I don't have you thrown in jail." The young man sneered. Rainwater turned and walked into the back of the restaurant. He walked over to a hand sink near the back door and started washing. The young man watched him for a moment, then followed him inside. "Just what the hell do you think you're doing? I told you to clear out." The man waved dramatically.

Rainwater looked up at the man. He splashed some water on his hands and pushed the soap dispenser deliberately. "If you're going to cheat an old man out of ten dollars, you're gonna at least let him clean up." Rainwater's face was tired looking, drawn.

"Cheat you? Oh no you don't." Mr. Shires reached for Rainwater's shirt, but he pulled away. The man glowered at him.

"I tell you what; you throw me out of here and I'm gonna walk straight around to the other side, garbage-covered clothes and all, and walk right through your restaurant telling everybody in there that you'd beat a poor, hungry man out of ten dollars. You decide." Rainwater stood with his back towards the sink. The man thought for a moment.

"I'll have you arrested," Mr. Shires threatened.

"So? I've been arrested before. It'd give me a place to sleep, as a matter of fact."

Mr. Shires scowled. "Okay, you clean up, then. But then you get on out of here. I've no need for trouble-makers, you hear?" He stomped away to the front of the restaurant. "And make it snappy," he called just before he walked through the door.

Rainwater turned back around and finished washing. The woman stood over her sink, quietly washing dishes. Finally, he dried his hands and arms and face on the roller beside the hand sink, picked up his bag stiffly, and stepped through the doorway.

The woman put her head through the doorway. "Hey mister." Rainwater turned around awkwardly, his joints barely bending. "You go on down to the corner an' wait," she said quickly, then she pulled her head back in.

Rainwater walked slowly through the growing darkness down the alleyway to the corner, silently cursing himself. She had been giving him clues just by the way she stopped singing and made more noise with the pots and pans, but he had been too inattentive to pick up on it. He stopped under the street lamp, made close by a soft fog that was beginning to roll in. He dropped his bag on the pavement and sat down slowly. His entire body ached. After a couple of minutes, the dishwasher came trotting down the alley with a large white sack in her hand. She ran over to him and handed him the sack.

"Here," she panted after her run. "It's some san'wiches an' slaw an' such. They're a little old maybe, they're from yesterday, but I figure they're better'n nothin'. Mr. Shires lets me take 'em home when they gets a day old, but my momma'll fix us somethin' when I get home." Rainwater peered into the sack. "I'm sorry, Mister. It's all I could get."

"No, no, this'll be great. Thank you." Rainwater closed the sack and looked up at the woman. "He gives you food to take home?" The dog from the beach that morning wandered towards them, trotting easily by the curb.

"Yeah, for me and momma, but it ain't right, him not payin' you an' all." She shook her head. "He oughta pay you. You done some nasty work an' he shouldn't be looking for some way to get out of payin' you ten mis'able dollars." The dog stopped short several paces from them and lowered his tail.

"Yeah, well, it's my own fault, I guess. I shoulda minded my own business." Rainwater bent over to stand, but his back balked at the effort. The woman reached down to help him up, but he waved her away. "No, it's okay. I'm not goin' anywhere." He dropped his hand to his lap. "You'd better get on back before he fires you too."

"Oh, he ain't firin' me." She stood with her hands on her hips. "I'm 'bout the best dishwasher he got, I guess. He ain't lettin' me go, no sir. Mm mm. No sir. He wouldn't fire me, 'cause then he'd haveta put me an' momma an' Treesha out an' he wouldn't do that, I don't think. But I am sorry what he did to you, mister. He ain't usually like that, really. Shoo!" She waved both hands at the dog who crouched now and gave her a pitiful look. "Shoo, dog."

Rainwater sat still under the sallow glow of the street lamp. He squinted up at the woman. "Maybe I'll just think of it as tuition." Rainwater leaned back on his pack and tried to relax. He could feel the muscles begin to stretch.

"Huh?" The woman grimaced at him. The dog sat very still, watching.

"Nothin'. It's just that there's always more goin' on than you ever really know. Kinda sounds like your Mr. Shires does try to help out some, doesn't it?"

"Well, I dunno." The young woman turned now and stood over Rainwater. "You s'pose all that hep gives me some of those choices you talkin' 'bout?" She looked at him for a moment, and Rainwater didn't know what to say. Then the dishwasher smiled sadly and shrugged. "That's what I thought." She motioned with her thumb. "I guess I'd better be goin' back."

"Yeah, I guess." Rainwater nodded. His body was tired and his head felt as if something had been removed from his thoughts, but he couldn't place it. He shook his head to try to remove the sensation as the woman turned. "But listen," he called suddenly, "if you ever get down to Florida, look me up, okay?"

The woman looked back at him and smiled. "I just might do that, Mister Drifter. I just might do that. But don't hold dinner on me." The woman turned then and trotted back down the alleyway. Rainwater watched her stop when she reached the doorway of the restaurant and look back at him sitting in the street, leaning against the light pole beside the amusement park. He dug into the sack and pulled out a soggy corned beef sandwich. The dog crept closer to him and he tore a corner off the sandwich and tossed it to the dog at the same time he bit into the rest of the sandwich. Rainwater watched the dog looking at him expectantly for another hand out. "You got your master to feed you, Zack. Go on home." Rainwater waved absently and the dog trotted away. "And I guess I have my own masters," Rainwater said to the space the dog had vacated. He took another bite of the hearty, salty sandwich.

In the Pines

You know, I did try. I wanted to do more and I wanted to be a good father. I didn't though. I didn't do more and I expect I was a lousy Dad, even when I was there. I mean, you know, before. The worst part is, how I left Carla, their Momma, to do everything when I gave up. And really, that's what I did. I gave up. Or ran away, which is the same thing, really. Funny. Carla always liked to say, 'Never, ever give up.' But I did and I guess she didn't. She's a better person than me, that's for sure. Wonder how she is.

The big truck ground to a stop, its air brakes letting out a gasp and a hiss. Rainwater tossed his bag out, and then climbed from the cab. It was very high off the ground and he had to be careful not to twist an ankle. He waved to the driver and slammed the surprisingly small door as he hopped off the truck.

"Thanks again," he called amidst the revving of the engine. The truck slowly started off in a blue-brown cloud of diesel fumes and road dust. Rainwater picked up his bag and slung it over his shoulder. The sun shone warm. The sky was very blue and Rainwater glanced around to see if there were any clouds at all. He had spent too many days walking in the rain recently. There were some clouds, off to the east a ways. The trees were still green, though it was winter, and Spanish moss gave a gray-green cast to the occasional live oaks. Rainwater walked along the highway. He turned on a small road, a sign saying it was the direction to Simonton. He walked along the road through the woods, which changed to pines and cedars. Occasionally there were hardwood trees, but mostly they were tall pine, with no branches low, just at the top. The deeper he walked into the woods, the less the sunlight reached the floor of the forest which was brown with needles. A wide path cut away from the road and Rainwater walked off the road and onto the path, letting the pastoral beauty of the path draw him away from the road. He thought about his days hiking with his shipmates along the trails in his youth. He had always pushed to the front of the gaggle of young men, leading them along the rocky paths. The sweet pine smell here reminded him of the trail from Las Lajas. Walking was easy on the wide flat trail covered with pine needles. It was dark under the trees. A breeze blew the tops of the trees, but did not blow on the bottom. Rainwater walked on the path until he came to a creek that flowed quickly but smoothly through the pine forest.

He walked beside the creek, where the trail now led. Then the creek slowed and in places spread, marsh-like. The trail grew harder to follow through the marsh. Sometimes, there seemed to be many trails. Perhaps they all lead to the same place, thought Rainwater. Then it was not so marshy, but the trail was gone. There was only the soft brown needle floor. Rainwater stopped under a bald cypress tree and sat, leaning up against the spreading trunk. He took a half sandwich out of his bag and unwrapped it. He could hear birds above him in the branches. I wish I had never taken that trail, he thought. But he was still next to the stream, so he could not be too lost. He could always go back to where he took the path, although there wasn't anything more back there where he had started really than there was here where he was. He reassured himself and finished his sandwich. He lit a cigarette and smoked it slowly. It was pleasant in the woods and he lingered. He wondered how long he had been walking. He could not see the sun. He decided he should start again so he stood and arched his back, threw the bag back over his shoulder and continued to follow the creek, though now it was slower walking without a trail. The stream began to curve more, so Rainwater cut the corners, always keeping the stream to his left and within sight, because it could turn away without his knowing it. He could hear the wind gathering in the tops of the trees, but it was still calm on the bottom. Sometimes in the strong wind he could look up and see sky. Clouds had blown up. It began to get cooler and darker. Rainwater decided he had best make a camp since either night was approaching or rain. He found a high spot in the middle of a horseshoe turn in the creek, which was moving very slowly. He took a long knife from his pack and walked to the stream. He could see the darkening sky and the threatening clouds above the water. Along the stream, he found some bushes and he cut long switches from them. Using heavier pine branches from the forest floor, he built a lean-to on the knoll. He put his raincoat over the top then covered it with pine-needles. He built up the bottom of the shelter with more pine needles and spread a tattered blanket over them. It was almost dark. A light rain began to fall and Rainwater climbed under his shelter. It was good, he thought. He was a bit proud of his bedraggled shelter. It did not leak much except at one edge where his coat did not reach. He made a little trough with his knife for the drip to run out. I'll put my feet at that end, he thought. Rainwater remembered taking his family camping, the girls giggling in the other side of the two-room tent he would set up. Rainwater put his bag under his head and listened to the gentle rain. The drops made a pleasant hiss as they hit the pine forest floor. Then he thought about the stream rising in the night. He hadn't thought about that. He tried to peer out between the pine branches but it was too dark and now it was raining even harder. If the creek flooded, he would be right in the middle of the water. He had been so foolish! "This is how it happens," he said aloud, his voice sounding oddly out of place in the steady roaring of the rain. This is how a man dies, he thought, but did not say aloud. Alone along some forgotten creek in South Carolina, washed downstream by a simple rain storm, perhaps washed out to sea, for all he knew where he might be. Ironic, he decided, that his final resting place could end up being the sea. He had been a sailor, after all. Then he caught himself up. "Don't do that," he admonished himself aloud. "You don't know where this stupid creek goes, and you aren't going to die." But his mind wouldn't stop the train of thought. He reminded himself he had been a strong swimmer, but wrapped up in a coat and all, who knew? His daughters would never know what happened to him . . .

"Damn!" Rainwater sat up now to stop the despair and, in doing so, pulled the raincoat back from the edge of the roofline he had made. A steady stream of water that had puddled on the coat ran down his back. He shivered and lay back on the now soggy blanket, listening to the rain, waiting for the creek to rise. He clenched his teeth and fell asleep.

Rainwater awoke to find his clothes soaked. He shivered, sat up and pushed back the branches he had stacked up. The creek was pretty much the same place it was before he had made his lean-to. He climbed from his shelter. It was morning, but he could not see the sun. He supposed it was very early. He walked to the stream and washed his face, taking a long drink of the cool water. He felt cold down to his bones. He took what was left of the shelter down and scattered the twigs and branches. He rolled the blanket and tried to squeeze the water out, but it was too threadbare to hold much water. Rainwater coughed, trying to move something deep in his chest, but it wouldn't break. He rolled his raincoat and shoved it into his soggy bag and started off. Nothing like being lost in the woods to make your day, Rainwater groused to himself. But it was a pleasant morning. Birds sang above him in the pines and cedars and palmettos. He followed the stream past a copse of trees. His arms felt clammy in his wet shirt sleeves. There was a bridge just beyond the next turn. Rainwater climbed the embankment next to the bridge. On the bridge, a sign said "Welcome to Simonton." Rainwater walked into the town. That close. Rainwater shook his head. He had been that close to a town. He stopped at the edge of the bridge, leaned over, and tried again to dislodge the heaviness in his chest with deep coughs.

Rainwater trudged across the bridge, a pickup truck whizzing past him without slowing. The stirring air from the vehicle made him quiver. He plodded along the edge of the road, looking over the town. There was a windshield shop, then a hair salon. Beyond those were some clapboard houses that had been converted into various professional offices: a dentist, a lawyer, an insurance agency. Still farther up, a parking lot had a half dozen cars and trucks parked in it. The sign read Bee's Diner. Rainwater headed for the food. He would beg one of the customers for their change. Offer to work, although his back hurt and he couldn't shake the feeling of penetrating cold. His throat tickled and he coughed but this time when he coughed, he couldn't stop and he found himself bending at the waist, trying to cough up the tickle and the block on his chest and trying not to cough. A large SUV sped past and Rainwater realized he was standing almost in the road, although the car had not slowed for him. He stepped to the side and something about the movement seemed to help the cough, but when he raised his head, he saw his vision turn to tiny dots and his head felt light and then it was black.

Rainwater awoke to see a young man standing over him in a blue medical shirt, leaning down and talking. Rainwater tried to figure out the words. " . . . okay? Nearly fell into the street . . ." He put his very cool hand on Rainwater's forehead. Rainwater stared straight up for a second. ". . . .burning up. We need to get you to a doctor . . ." Rainwater pushed away his fogginess. He thought this fellow was a doctor.

"Wait. What?" Rainwater raised his head and felt it throbbing. There was a woman standing behind the man in the medical shirt. She had on scrubs as well.

"Hold on, sir. We'll get you an ambulance." Another woman showed up behind the other two. She held a cellphone to her ear.

"Yeah, on Poplar Street, right in front of Doctor Parker's office," the woman spoke to the phone. "Just fell out, maybe hit his head, we don't know."

"No, his head isn't hurt, I don't think." The man was groping around the back of Rainwater's head now. Rainwater felt like a mannequin or something. Now there was a small crowd, maybe six people, standing over him. They seemed to be all speaking at once.

" . . .seen him before?"

" . . .car didn't even slow down . . ."

" . . . might have been killed . . ."

" . . . they'd be here in ten minutes . . ."

" . . .fever . . ."

"Wait. I'm okay." Rainwater protested but in fact he wasn't at all certain he was okay. But he didn't want to go to a hospital. He had a deep fear he would go in and never come out. Seemed to him, people of his background did not do well in hospitals. And he had never had to go to doctors much. Although never a big man, he had always been strong, sinewy. Rainwater managed to sit up and the folks around him grew quieter. A couple walked away, either satisfied he was all right, or disappointed. Rainwater sat in the gravel beside the road and gathered his thoughts. The man in scrubs stooped down next to him.

"Are you sure you're okay? You kind of fell like a tree." He reached over and grabbed Rainwater by the arm and pulled him up. He felt very strong to Rainwater and Rainwater felt a bit like a ragdoll. He stood wobbly for a moment, looked around him and felt his head start to spin again.

"Whoa. I need to sit for a second." Rainwater looked around him. The man half lead him, half carried him over to the front stoop of a clapboard office. The sign in the yard said

Samuel B. Parker, DMS in an elegant scroll. Rainwater jabbed his thumb in the direction of the sign as they passed it. "You?"

"Yeah. Here, sit here on the steps until the EMTs get here." Rainwater allowed himself to be planted on the steps of the building.

Rainwater half sat, half fell to the step and the dentist pulled out his cell phone. Rainwater wanted to protest, but somehow didn't feel like he had the energy to. Then he coughed repeatedly, saw the dots in his vision again and he felt the world go dizzy, then black.

Rainwater woke up in a curtained off room, the smell of disinfectants and deodorizers filling his nostrils. A woman was writing on a clipboard and talking to someone at the same time. It took a moment for Rainwater to realize she was talking to him.

" . . .may be pneumonia but we will need to do an x-ray to be sure . . ." she was saying.

"Wait." Rainwater made a feeble attempt to rise but found he could raise his head and maybe his shoulders a bit, but anything more just wouldn't happen. The woman looked up from her clipboard and placed her hand on his chest to keep him lying down, although it was hardly necessary. Rainwater started another coughing spell that he could barely stop. His head hurt.

"Stay calm, sir. We're going to take good care of you." She looked around her. "Julie? I need you here a moment." She turned back to look down at Rainwater. "You'll be fine, sir." A young black woman now stood beside the woman.

"Yes, Doctor?" Julie was looking at Rainwater too, and he wondered what she saw, but she gave nothing away.

"What happened?" Rainwater thought about trying to stand but quickly dismissed it. "Where am I?" He managed to turn his head enough to see the arms of the gurney he was in, the shiny rod next to that with a bag on it, and then he traced with his eyes the tube that led from that to his arm. "Oh."

"You're okay," Julie smiled now.

The doctor was talking too, but not to Rainwater. " . . .need a CT scan and CBC. " The doctor spun and walked away.

"Yes, ma'am," Julie said but the doctor was gone.

"Where am I?" Rainwater felt his senses getting some better. "What have you got me on?" He glanced again at the plastic bag on the tower.

"Just hydration." Julie tucked in an already tight corner and pushed the gurney through the door and into the hallway. "You are at Harton County Medical. You had a pretty good spill there." She pushed the gurney through a set of swinging metal doors. "How you feeling?" She watched the sides of the gurney and pushed.

"Better, I think." But the stream of fluorescent lights going past his head made him a little disoriented. "Am I sick?" he managed as he closed his eyes. "Where's my stuff?" Rainwater coughed heavily.

"I wondered if you were able to hear her. You were pretty woozy when you came in. You got pneumonia, most likely, and you were dehydrated from that fever." She pushed him into a lab and stopped. "You remember Doctor Parker? Brought you in?"

"Yeah." Rainwater watched as Julie moved around the room.

"He said he's got your stuff for you at his office."

"What? I need my stuff. He can't keep my things."

Julie stopped fussing around the room. "Now, you think he wants your old stuff? Really!" She went back to her preparations.

Rainwater considered it for a moment. "No, I suppose not. But still, it's mine."

"Well, he might've saved your life. You were one sick puppy. Yes sir. One sick puppy." She scooted him to a table and a man came in and the two of them picked him up and slid him onto a table. Rainwater realized then he had on only a hospital gown and he wondered how that happened, exactly. The two picked him up so easily, it made Rainwater feel small. Was he really that easy to pick up? The two of them talked in quiet tones, then Julie came to Rainwater's side. "We're gonna slide you into this machine. Lie very still and don't move, okay?" Rainwater considered if he even felt like he could move, then nodded. Julie patted his chest. "Okay. Tom here will take over." And Julie was gone.

When the scan was finished, Rainwater was pushed down the hall again, but this time they stopped at a room and put him in a bed. Rainwater felt like he was watching all this happen to someone else. They took his name, but rarely addressed him by it. Nurses came and took his temperature and felt his pulse and left with barely a word. It went by in a blur. Meanwhile, Rainwater slept except when he coughed. But mostly, he lay in a warm, dry bed with clean sheets and slept. Sure, it was a hospital bed, but it sure beat any other bed he had had for a long time. And that evening, they brought him a meal. Meatloaf, green beans, and cottage cheese with peaches. Rainwater tried to eat it all, but he was unaccustomed to the portions and got full.

The first time Rainwater got up to use the toilet, he stopped in front of a mirror long enough to see he was far thinner than he realized he had gotten. He had been a strapping young man, then a wiry but powerful middle aged man. But when he looked at the gaunt reflection in the mirror, he saw a stranger's face. He pulled up his gown and saw his ribs, his bony knees, his hip bones. His beard was grey, scraggly, and his hair was a white mess. He looked back at his face in the mirror accusatively, as if to say to himself, "How did you let yourself get this way?"

Rainwater slept off and on for the next day. He turned the television on and tried to watch the shows, but he didn't know any of the story lines, and he didn't want to watch the news, so he just left it on a low volume to provide some noise other than the garbled intercom announcements and the clanking of equipment. Nurses came in and took his temperature and pulse, but always seemed to be in a rush. There was a young man who brought the food tray that night, and he was pleasant enough, but he too seemed to be heading out the door as quickly as he came in. Mostly, Rainwater sat in the bed, watching people go into the other rooms, families, perhaps, visiting sick relatives. Or friends. Sometimes he heard awkward laughter coming from the rooms, and he heard one skinny man stand in the doorway of a room saying, "You'd do anything to get out of work, wouldn't you?" Rainwater winced when he heard the young man say it. Rainwater thought he tried not to listen to these other patients joking about their ailments, or comforting those who had come to the hospital to see them. But the truth was Rainwater didn't have anyone come by to see him so he listened intently. Mostly, he sat alone, almost a skeleton of the man he had been, watching glimpses of other people's lives through the angle of the doorway, down a narrow hallway. When the nurse came by and closed the door for the evening, he felt completely closed in, shut off from the lives of these strangers he had watched come in or leave.

Nurse Julie did stop by the next morning. Rainwater had just finished his breakfast and he was trying to recall the last time he had had both supper one night and breakfast the next morning. Julie came in with a big smile on her face, looked at the chart at the end of his bed, fiddled a bit with the hoses that led to his arm, and asked him how he was. Rainwater was glad to have the company and he tried to strike up a conversation, but he didn't have much to talk to her about. After a few minutes, Julie patted his very thin arm and said, "I think they're getting you all fixed up. I've got something I want to do for you."

"What's that?"

"Can I cut your hair? Give you a shave? You'd feel a lot better."

Rainwater thought it over for a moment. "Yeah, sure. Why not?"

Julie cut his hair as he lay in the bed, trying not to move except when she sat him up to cut the back. Then she cut his beard back and shaved his chin using a can of shave cream and a disposable razor she had brought. The warm water on his face when she finished felt odd. He rubbed his smooth chin and it felt very strange to him.

"Thank you." He managed a smile, but he wondered what he must look like, clean shaven, hair cut back. But he did feel better for it, somehow.

"Well, it's not as good as my sister can do, but it'll have to do." And then she smiled and left and Rainwater knew she was not coming back. After she was gone, Rainwater walked his IV tower to the bathroom and looked in the mirror again. This time, he saw vaguely the man he had once seen in his photos, or, rather, the photos he had left behind, but he was so much thinner, so frail looking. Rainwater returned to his bed and climbed back in, but it seemed harder to do after seeing his aged face, as if seeing how decrepit he looked had sapped his strength. He sat in his bed, the fluorescent lights buzzing above him. The man who was in the room across from him was wheeled out in a wheelchair, his lap full of flowers. A woman walked beside him, a purse on her arm, her eyes on the long white cast on the man's leg.

Rainwater watched the movement of characters on the television, the sound turned so low he could only hear them murmur indistinct mumbles, interspersed with suddenly dramatic music. A man in a white coat walked in briefly and asked Rainwater to sign a form, something about indigent care, and then spun on his heels and walked out without fanfare. It seemed quieter in the hallway this day. Rainwater was watching the clock, waiting for lunch, when a doctor came in, dressed in scrubs, a stethoscope around her neck. A nurse came with her and fiddled with the bed sheets.

"How are you feeling, Mister . . ." the doctor paused, looking at the chart.

"Rainwater, folks call me Rainwater. I'm feeling much better. Thanks." He tried to manage a smile, but it just didn't feel natural, so he gave it up.

"You gave us a bit of a scare there, Mr. Rainwater." The doctor looked up from the clipboard and handed it to the nurse who was standing beside her now. "Let me hear you take a big breath." The doctor put the stethoscope into her ears and leaned over Rainwater. He took in as big a breath as he could and let it out. "Yeah, better." The doctor gave a nod to the nurse who wrote something on the chart. "I think you're doing much better."

"Thank you." Rainwater wasn't sure why he thanked her, as if doing better was his accomplishment, but it seemed to satisfy her.

"You ready to get out of here?" The doctor stood over Rainwater, her face impassive. Rainwater thought again about the lunch that was likely on its way, then shrugged.

"Yeah, sure. Um, maybe after lunch?"

The doctor broke into a grin. "After lunch it is." She started for the door and then stopped. "You have someone we should call? Where will you go when we release you?"

"No, no one to call." Rainwater shook his head. "I'll be fine."

The doctor looked at the nurse. "Call discharge planning." Then to Rainwater, she said, "You're better, but you're not well. You need to take a few days." Then she was out the door.

After lunch, a young woman came in with a clipboard. "Mr. Rainwater?" She held the clipboard close to her.

"Well, really just Rainwater, but I'll answer to most any-thing." Rainwater felt suddenly very tired. There were so many questions, and he worried about the questions.

"We are going to release you in a little bit. You have any place to go? Do you have anyone I should call?"

"No. No. There's no one." Rainwater let a weight settle in on him. "No. No one. Just let me go. I'll be fine."

"Well, how will you care for yourself? Do you have a place? An apartment or even a room?" She looked at the clipboard now, lifted the top page and dropped it.

"No, I've been taking care of myself a long time. I'm fine. I just need my stuff. That dentist fellow, he's got it. I'm okay on my own."

"Yes, Dr. Parker, I believe." She glanced absently at the clipboard then nodded. "I'll give him a call. Thank you."

"I just need my stuff . . ." but she was out the door, walking down the hallways with a click-click of her shoes. Rainwater lay still for a few minutes. The floor was quiet today. It almost seemed like he was the only patient there. He got out of bed and sat in the chair for a few minutes, but with only the gown on, he felt conspicuous. He wished he had his clothes. He'd bust out of this place. When he stood to return to his bed, he saw his bent over body in the mirror again. He was 58, but he looked like he was 90. He stared at himself in the mirror, tried to straighten his back and stand taller, but it made no difference. He was old, somehow. Old and frail and at the mercy of others.

Just as Rainwater returned to his bed, Dr. Parker stuck his head into the doorway and knocked on the partially open door. "Mr. Rainwater?" He smiled into the darkness of Rainwater's room. "You up for some company?"

"It's just 'Rainwater.' Sure. You got my stuff?

"Yes sir, I do. My sons helped me bring it. Can they come in?"

Just then two towheaded boys stood in the doorway as well, their arms full of Rainwater's pack and another bag Rainwater didn't recognize. Rainwater waved them in. How else could he get his stuff?

The dentist pointed to a space next to the doorway where a stiff hospital chair was pushed up squarely against the wall. "Just put it there, boys." The dentist came over to the bed but the two boys, who looked to be maybe 8 or 9 stood cautiously by the doorway. "How are you feeling?"

"I'm okay." Rainwater felt the questioning beginning to wear on him. "They say I can leave today."

Dr. Parker raised his eyebrows. "Oh! Well! Congratulations! You hear that, boys? Mr. Rain . . ., Rainwater here gets to leave today." He half turned to his sons, evidently trying to draw them into the conversation, although Rainwater couldn't imagine why.

"Dad? You tell him we did a search for him?" The older boy stepped closer. The dentist started a little.

Rainwater felt his head grow hot fast. "What?" Rainwater let a deep scowl fall over his face. "What? What kind of search?"

"Just an internet . . ." The boy stepped backwards.

"We were just trying to help . . ." The dentist stiffened his back as well.

"You had no right," Rainwater snapped. "You might find out what you don't ever need to know. Mind your own . . ." Then Rainwater stopped. "What did you find?"

"Oh, nothing, really." The dentist stumbled for words.

"It's a German name." The older boy chimed in. "Seth thought you were a native American, but we found out it's from Germany."

"I didn't say he was native American," Seth offered from the doorway.

"That's enough, boys." Dr. Parker held his hand flat to his side and the boys fell silent. "We weren't prying. They just liked your name, sir."

"Oh." Rainwater looked away. "You got my stuff there?" He looked back at the pile in the chair.

"Yes sir," Seth mumbled.

"Do an old man a favor and bring me my clothes?"

Seth and his brother grabbed Rainwater's duffle bag and plopped it on the end of the bed, although Rainwater could barely recognize it. It was clean now, and much fuller. "Thank you. I get to leave in a bit and I need to get dressed." Rainwater tried to soften his tone. He didn't want to be the scary old man.

The boys stepped back again. "Where are you going?" The dentist repositioned the duffle bag absently.

"I don't know. South."

"Can I give you bus fare? It's hard to travel like you do anymore."

Rainwater waved his hand. "No, you've done too much already." He pursed his lips at his unintended double meaning. "I'll be fine. Thank you." This time his voice was gentler. "Buses, they get checked . . ." he stopped. "Thank you, Dr. Parker. You probably saved my life."

"You're welcome, Mister, er, I mean, Rainwater."

"And thank you boys for helping out an old man." The two boys shuffled back and forth.

When the dentist and his sons left, Rainwater pulled the duffle bag up and looked inside, but his clothes were not there. Instead, there were new clothes, and several of everything: jeans, khaki work pants, a denim work shirt, cotton shirts with pockets on the chest, lots of socks, underwear, even a sweatshirt with Coker College written on it. Rainwater looked at the doorway where they had left, then picked out a pair of khaki pants and a cotton shirt. When he was dressed, he marveled at the feeling of new clothes, clothes that still had some substance left. He went over to the chair and looked in the other bag. His blanket was there, but so were a tightly rolled sleeping bag and a small tent and even some toiletries. It felt like Christmas to Rainwater and he blinked back watery eyes. A knock came on the door but it opened before he could respond. A burly man with a wheelchair pushed through the doorway.

"You ready, sir?"

Rainwater gathered his new belongings.

Red's Ribs and Bar-B-Q

I saw a calf one time that had two faces. Not two heads, mind you, but two faces. Strangest thing you ever saw. Two mouths, two tongues, four eyes but everything from the face back was normal. All he could do was walk in circles. Farmer sold him to a carnival not long after it was born. Guess folks will pay to see something like that. He was strange to see.

Rainwater smelled Reds Ribs and Bar-B-Q long before he saw it. The wood smoke was unmistakable. But when he walked up to the hand lettered sign, there was not much to see. A simple cinderblock building supported a rusted metal roof that had been patched with seemingly random cutouts of tin. A piece of plywood painted white with red hand-lettering was the total of the advertising. A dirt parking lot held a smattering of pickup trucks, hard-driven sedans, and a large SUV with a bulldog sticker on the bumper. Hickory smoke permeated the area. Rainwater thought about the money he had found in his pack left by the doctor and the children, a hand-stitched wallet with a change purse inside. There were four crumpled singles and $2.15 in coins in the wallet. He knew it had to come from one of the boys. A part of him wished he had stayed in Simonton. But he didn't belong there. He knew, what, four people there? Maybe five? And what would he have done if he had stayed? No, he was right to move on. And he decided a barbecue sandwich purchased with the money from his benefactors would be a worthy use for that gift. Since he had left South Carolina the week before, he had eaten only sparingly, saving his resources tightly. He had eaten half a hamburger left on a table outside a burger place when he saw the teenager grab his cell phone and run off with his friends. He had gnawed on some under-ripe peaches from an unkempt orchard that gave him an intense stomach ache a half hour later. One morning he had a biscuit begged from the early cook at a diner in Newington. The funny thing was, eating three meals a day in the hospital had made him get hungry all the faster once he was back on the road. But here he was, back on the road, and eating once a day, if he could.

When he came into Red's, there were four men with baseball caps seated in the center of the room at one of the smattering of red Formica topped tables with chrome and scratched green plastic chairs around them. Their conversation stopped as Rainwater came in and walked past them. He slid in a wooden booth along one wall, putting his packs on the inside. He couldn't help but notice the four sets of eyes follow him as he crossed the room, but he pretended he hadn't noticed. He was accustomed to being the stranger no one recognized. In fact, it was what he chose. In just a moment, a very large man with a white apron stained with barbecue sauce and dark grease stood next to Rainwater's booth, wiping his hands absently on a tattered cloth. He seemed put out that a customer had come in.

"What for you?" His hair was cropped close and he squinted when he asked the question.

"Can I see a menu please?" Rainwater winced under his glare. The man simply jerked his thumb toward the wall where a cola sign told the menu. "Oh, well, um, I'll guess I'll have a pork sandwich, please, with pickles and onions and, well, I guess that's it." Rainwater counted the coins in his head. He had plenty for that.

"What to drink?" Rainwater suddenly realized everyone else in the place was quiet.

"Oh, uh, water please."

"All right. Hold on." The man turned and trudged off. One of the four men held his beer bottle up as the burly man walked past them.

"Red? Four more?" Red simply nodded.

"Naw, I can't Jimmy, . . ." One younger man started scooting back from the table. He was sinewy, spare. He wore jeans and a white tee shirt.

"I insist, Bobby Lee. My treat." Bobby Lee sat down again, looking a bit sheepish.

"Oh. Okay. Thanks, Jimmy." Jimmy nodded. Jimmy was smaller, older, with jet black hair combed back, and although he also wore jeans, his shirt was a neatly-pressed blue oxford.

Rainwater could hear a pinball machine in an adjacent room bing-binging along. They still had pinball? Rainwater looked down at the table before him, not making eye contact with the four men and they eventually resumed a conversation they had evidently been in. They spoke loudly and Rainwater couldn't help but overhear them. Rainwater studied the names carved into the wooden table top of the booth. Initials and dates testified to various comings and goings. Someone evidently graduated from a LCHS the year before. Hearts with initials vowed love for now anonymous diners.

Bobby Lee shifted in his seat, nervous. "Like I was saying, I can't make no money off a them onions. I'll tell you what, Jimmy. I don't know what to do when nobody wants to buy any onions anymore." Bobby Lee wagged his head, staring at his empty beer bottle. Red placed the beers he had carried over by the necks and placed them before the men. "I just can't sell them anymore even if I could bring them in, which I can't because there's no one who wants to work no more." Bobby Lee picked up a bottle and took a long draw from it.

"Oh sure you can sell onions, Bobby Lee. Everybody eats onions." Jimmy turned his bottle up for a quick drink. "You can't make anything doesn't have onions in it. Look at any recipe you see, odds are good it's got onions in it."

"Yeah, but you know how that goes. People don't want to pay for the good stuff. They want those cheap onions from Guatemala. They don't want to pay what it costs me to grow them." Bobby Lee took another long drink. The other two men watched back and forth, as if sizing up the conversation.

"Well, everyone knows we grow the best onions in the world down here. You wait. It'll be okay. Won't it, Scott?"

The man next to him raised his beer bottle. "Best there is, Jimmy." He took a short drink. He eyed Bobby Lee closely. He was bigger, heavier, older than Bobby Lee. He wore tired overalls and a faded yellow tee shirt.

"Yeah, I hear what you're saying. I don't know. But I'm running out of patience. I'm telling you I can't get anyone to harvest them. I'm ready to try something new, something different." Bobby Lee stared at his bottle then looked up at Scott. "I'm thinking maybe about growing cotton next year. What do you think about cotton, Scott?"

"Cotton?" Scott and the man opposite him said in unison.

"Hell, Bobby Lee. You can't grow cotton any easier than you can onions." Scott leaned heavily on the table. "You'd have to have all new equipment to do that. You can't switch now. Why in the world would you . . ."

"Maybe the bank . . ." Bobby Lee looked up at Jimmy.

Jimmy crossed his arms on the table and leaned forward and Bobby Lee stopped. "You need to stick with the onions, Bobby Lee." It sounded more like an order than a suggestion. Rainwater was lost in listening to the conversation and was startled to see Red at the edge of his table holding a sandwich wrapped in white paper and a couple of small Styrofoam bowls with pickles and onions in them.

"Oh! Thank you!" Rainwater wondered if it was obvious he was eavesdropping. Red stood stolid before him, emotionless.

"Anything else?"

"Uh, water?"

"Hold on." Red trudged back to the kitchen. The pinball machine stopped clanging in the back. Rainwater unwrapped the sandwich and placed several layers of onions and pickles on it. He carefully replaced the top and took a bite. The smoky, salty flavor was unmistakable. A boy came from the back and stood now next to Bobby Lee.

"Dad? Can I have some more quarters?"

"Water." Red said evenly, and slid the red plastic tumbler onto the table and tossed a wrapped straw next to it.

"Oh. Thanks." Rainwater tried to sound friendly, but he was not getting any reaction. He wished he still had his long white hair. For some reason, people seemed to react well to that. But no, he had short if unkempt hair and four days' beard, so he looked perhaps even rougher than he did before, if that was possible. He took another bite and chewed slowly, savoring.

"No, Dallis. That's all for today." But the boy wasn't looking at his father, but over at Rainwater, where Red had just walked away.

"Daddy?"

"You know, Jimmy, I might be able to get some used equipment . . ."

"Daddy?"

"No, Bobby Lee. You can't. You can't afford it." Jimmy looked over at the boy and softened his tone.

"Daddy?"

"What?"

"Who's that man?" Dallis was pointing unabashedly at Rainwater. The men turned and looked at Rainwater. He felt like a sideshow or something.

Bobby Lee turned back around. "Don't you worry about him. He's only a stranger." He took another long drink from his beer then lowered his bottle. "He'll be moving on soon enough. Probably just a drifter. Don't point at people" He placed the nearly empty bottle on the table and glanced at Rainwater.

"What's a drifter?" The boy was still staring at Rainwater, but he had at least dropped his arm and was no longer pointing at him. Rainwater went back to his sandwich and took another bite, this one smaller. He wanted the sandwich to last as long as he could make it last, but he also felt suddenly unwelcome.

"It means he's just a guy passing through. Leave him alone and stop gawking at him." Rainwater was at least glad for that. Bobby Lee returned to his conversation. "Jimmy, thing about onions is, I just can't get the help I need. I can't bring those onions in by myself and no one around here will do it." The two quieter men glanced up at each other, a look between them. "Cotton is mechanized. I can do that almost entirely with my tractors."

"Bobby Lee, it just won't work. Come by the office and we can talk about it if you want, okay? But you can't buy all new equipment." Jimmy spoke more softly now and looked intently at the wrapper of his beer bottle he had started peeling.

Scott chimed in, "Bobby Lee, stick with the onions. Now I got a crew over my place came in from down around Americus I can let you use for a few days. They can harvest most anything, I 'spect. That'll give me time to get my equipment set up."

Jimmy perked up. "There you go! That's a solution if I ever heard one." He reached over and slapped Scott on the shoulder and gave him an approving look. "That's the ticket."

Bobby Lee set his mouth in a straight line. "Scott, that's real good of you, but I . . ."

"I've already got them on my payroll, Bobby Lee. It's no big deal. You can pay me back once you sell those onions. No problem. In fact, it'll help me out, give them something to work on 'til I'm ready next week."

The fourth man finally spoke, his voice gravelly. "Know what, Bobby Lee? I got some fellows coming in too, as soon as the peaches are ready. They're picking cucumbers now, I think down around Perry. I'll send some on over if you need them. They'll work hard, if you got the volume."

Jimmy let out a big guffaw. "Hot damn, George, that's the deal! See, Bobby Lee? You don't need to throw in the towel on those onions. We got you covered. Hot damn."

Rainwater ate towards the end of his sandwich. Bobby Lee sat in his chair, looking from face to face at the men at the table around him. "Fellas, I'm . . . I just . . . I don't know what to say." Then he looked at his son who was now standing close to him, taking in the conversation.

"Say 'Yes'," Jimmy offered, smiling.

Bobby Lee began nodding his head slowly. "Yes. And thank you." He looked intently at the faces of Scott and George. "Yes, I would definitely use the help."

"Hot damn. That's what I'm talking about. One more, fellows?"

"Thanks, Jimmy. But I gotta drive. Got my boy here and we have to get back to the house." Bobby Lee pushed back and stood to leave. "Guys, I can't tell you what this means." Bobby Lee took off his cap and set his mouth in a tight line, holding the cap with both hands at his waist. The two men mumbled and waved him away, seeming to be embarrassed by his gratitude. Bobby Lee stepped away. "I'll call you, Scott." He and Dallis turned towards the door.

"You know what? You're right, Bobby Lee. I don't need another beer either. I need to get on back to the bank myself." Jimmy scooted his chair back. "Hey, Bobby Lee." Bobby Lee turned to look back and flipped his cap back on. "We're all family around here. You know that. We take care of our own. You'll be okay." Bobby Lee gave him a quick nod and a smile as he walked out the door with his son.

The other two men stood also. "Yeah, we gotta go too. We're going over to that service for Joe. You coming, Jimmy?" Scott removed his cap and pushed back his hair with the same hand and put his cap back on.

Jimmy looked at his wrist watch. "I can't. Meeting." The three remaining men walked up to the counter, tossed bills before Red, who said nothing, and left. Then Red walked into the back of the restaurant and Rainwater sat in the booth, the place quiet now except for the hum from a refrigerator somewhere in the back. Suddenly, the high-pitched whine of a saw broke the quiet, brief screeches repeated over and over as Red cut through rib bones in the back. Rainwater had finished his sandwich and now ate the last of the pickles and onions in the tiny bowls and then drank the pickle juice. He drank the last of his water and realized he had no more reason to stay, not that he had any reason to leave. His bill had been placed under the sandwich when Red had left it, so Rainwater counted out his money carefully into his right hand, scooted out of the booth, and grabbed his packs with his left hand. He crossed over to the wooden countertop where the cash register stood. Red came out of the back, scowling. Rainwater put the bill on the counter top with his carefully counted money and tried to give Red a sincere, needy look, but Red simply grabbed the money, dropped the coins in the register, and slammed it shut.

"Mighty good barbecue, sir." Rainwater crossed his hands before him, a posture he knew people found less threatening, earnest.

"Thanks." Red snorted. He leaned on his knuckles on the counter.

"Um" Rainwater tried to catch Red's focus, but he was expressionless and seemed focused somewhere twenty feet through Rainwater's head. "You know anyone needs some work done around here? I'm looking for day work." He thought about the farmers at the table, but he knew he could not hold his own harvesting in the fields. Red's eyes finally seemed to land on Rainwater. He gave him a quick squint.

"No."

"I'm pretty handy . . ."

"No, there ain't no jobs here for ya." Red stood solid as a wall, obviously waiting for Rainwater to leave, as if he might steal the giant peppermints from next to the cash register.

"It's just that folks here seem nice and . . ."

"No, there ain't no jobs. You move on now." Red waved towards the door with one massive hand. "Go on." He said it firmly but not aggressively. Rainwater sighed and picked up his bags from the floor next to him and walked out. They took care of their own, but he wasn't one of them.

The parking lot was empty now except for one battered pickup truck. Rainwater trudged down the highway, sticking his thumb out when vehicles came by, but no one stopped, and most of the cars looked like they were full of people anyway. Rainwater kept walking, his packs weighing on his shoulder, heading south.

The Celebration

My mother always told me things happen for a reason and I think she held that over from her religious upbringing but there's some truth to it, I think. Now, she meant everything happens for a reason and I don't necessarily believe that. I don't think tornados happen for a reason. I think they just happen and then folks have to deal with the destruction. But I think how people respond to a tornado happens for a reason. Everything people do is caused by some previous decision or opinion. Everything people do is for a reason. That's what momma should've said.

Rainwater lugged his packs along the state road. It would have been easier to get a ride on the US highway, but he worried about the state troopers and sheriff cars cruising through those routes. It was time for young people on break to be travelling, Rainwater figured, and the police would likely be on speeding patrol on the highways. So here he was, traipsing down a state route, his packs, heavier now with his recent gifts from the dentist and his sons, bending towards Florida. Or maybe he was heading towards Brunswick. He couldn't be sure exactly where this road would lead. But he was heading towards sand, that much he knew. If he could find a beach somewhere, a place to walk along the surf again, maybe he would be better able to forget. Maybe he could rid himself of the nagging doubts he felt.

To be a skinny state road, the traffic was surprisingly heavy, with a steady stream of cars and trucks rumbling past him. He walked on, his thumb held up over his shoulder, but no one stopped. That was the problem with a back road. He rarely got rides with local people. His rides usually came from truckers, maybe occasionally college kids, or a salesperson. He didn't think he looked threatening, but he knew he looked scruffy, at least, with his sagging coat, too warm today in the Georgia sun, and his shaggy crop of white hair under a beat up, twisted old cotton fedora. He probably wouldn't pick himself up as a hitchhiker, he thought. He smirked at his thoughts. It's a long way to Florida. He debated weeding out his packs to lighten them, but as he sorted through it in his mind, he couldn't think of anything he would not miss. His few clothes, his sleeping bag, which he had already found to be welcome over the thread-bare blanket he had before, and the small tent the dentist had given him, which had kept him dry several times now. No, there was not much to lose out of his packs.

Maybe it was him. Maybe he was just getting too old, too tired, too worn out for the road. Another sedan hummed past him, full of older people except for the driver, who looked younger. They didn't slow down or even seem to notice Rainwater trudging along the road.

As he topped a slow hill, Rainwater saw most of the cars turning onto a side road. He kept walking. By the time he got to the road, one Elkhorn Tavern Road the sign told him, four more cars had turned down it, so Rainwater did too. A half mile ahead, across from a tiny brick church, the cars were pulling off the road into a gravel lot and onto the shoulder of the road itself. The church parking lot looked like it was already full. Rainwater trudged towards the church, climbed a small hillside, and surveyed a gathering of people.

There were sixty or seventy people assembled. There was a metal-topped meeting area, post and beam, with a floor of crushed limestone and a few weeds. Folding chairs were lined up in rows under the metal roof, followed by uneven groupings of lawn chairs and blankets that spread out behind the structure towards the road. The shelter was down in a little valley, surrounded by black gums and pecan trees and pin oaks. Up the hill on the other side of the meeting area was a cemetery full of gravestones with the names of those who had passed before. Flowers graced some of the markers. Others looked dark, stained. People milled around in the gathering area, talking to each other, nodding. Some patted each other on the back gently, said a few words, wagged their heads, but it was all done in a slow, methodical pace. No one moved quickly except for a man with long brown hair, wearing a brown suit, who bustled about some speakers and microphones that were set up at one end of the shelter. An electric piano was sitting at one side, several amplifiers to the other. Rainwater dropped his packs and sat on the near hillside next to the church, away from the people, watching. More people came and parked in disarray along the side of the road. Then Rainwater noticed that a casket rested at the far end of the structure. He hadn't seen it at first because it was covered with flowers. A man and a woman came and stood in front of the casket and the others rose from their seats, lined up along one side of the rows of chairs, and made their way to the couple, one by one, shaking the couple's hands, first the woman and then the man. The woman, dressed in black, her blonde hair cut close, nodded, spoke a few words, shook a hand, then met the next person. The man did the same. He wore a black suit also, as well as a deep frown. The line moved slowly. Rainwater observed from his perch along the hill. At one point, the woman looked away, lost in a thought perhaps, maybe just tired, and her eyes rested on Rainwater for just a moment. He could see her blink, perhaps wondering if this was someone familiar or not. Then she returned to shaking hands and nodding, both consoling and being consoled, it appeared. The line wended its way along one side of the rows of chairs. Rainwater sat down in the grass and watched the group of people shuffling forward, followed with his eyes a flock of starlings as they flew across the open sky in a small murmuration, and let his focus fade as the trees swayed gently in a light breeze. He could have easily slipped into a nap.

After a while, the line grew shorter and a group of musicians started tuning up guitars, mandolins, and bass guitars in chairs behind the coffin. Rainwater returned from his reverie. The electric piano tinkled with trial notes. A microphone buzzed a short electrical hiss, then the muffled sounds of the people was punctuated by a broadcast, "Test. Two. Three." The same fellow in the brown suit fidgeted with the cords, twisted knobs on a black box, then stood behind one of the microphones with a guitar slung across his chest. A man with a Bible clutched close to his breast in his left hand walked up to a different microphone and raised his right hand. The crowd of people murmured down to quiet. The couple who had stood greeting well-wishers moved to the front row of the chairs.

"If I may have your attention, please," although the crowd had already grown quiet. "Please join me in prayer." He lowered his head, raised his right hand higher, and leaned into the microphone. Everyone else bowed their heads too, except Rainwater, who pulled one of his packs behind him and leaned against it. "Dear Lord, we just want to thank you for this opportunity to gather in your name to send your child Joe back to you," the preacher prayed. "We know that Joe didn't always get it right, but in the end, he did get right with you, Lord." A few bowed heads nodded in the crowd. "We just pray that his soul, resting now in your sacred bosom, is finally at ease, finally able to find the rest he deserves, the peace he searched for." More heads nodded. "Dear Lord, we beseech thee to hear our prayers and to bless this congregation that humbly meets before you and begs your forgiveness for all of our many sins. And we ask in the name of thy blessed son, Jesus Christ our Lord and Savior. Amen." The bowed heads looked up now. After a brief pause, the preacher continued, "We all knew Joe as a kind and considerate man, a fun-loving guy, but we all knew him mainly as a gifted musician. Joe took a great many roads to find his way home. But throughout his many travels, he kept his music, and he shared his music. I believe music was Joe's purpose, and I think he came to know that himself, that his wandering ways were just a way for him to keep his purpose in mind. Just as we must keep our own purpose in mind. Many is the time I heard Joe sing songs of glory. His ability to bring us all together was a true gift. He brightened all of our lives with his songs and . . ." A guitar chord broke loud and the preacher started. Some in the crowd tittered at his jump. He turned and looked at the long-haired man in the brown suit, then scooted off from the rows of chairs filled with people. Rainwater smirked. But he also thought about all these people out in the middle of nowhere meeting to pay tribute to this man named Joe. How many of these people had been touched by Joe's music? It made Rainwater wonder just what this Joe might have been like.

The long-haired man in the brown coat bounced just a moment on the balls of his feet. "I'm Jim. Becky and I want to thank you for coming." He paused and nodded towards the woman in the front row who had been greeting people. "Of all the things that made Joe happy, music was the one we shared the most. Joe never went anywhere without his guitar. He always had a song. We want to make music one more time with Joe." He glanced over to the casket then dipped his head to the other two musicians who were with him. The piano tinkled out a few notes, the bass came in, then Jim strummed and thumb picked the guitar and broke into "Sunday Morning Coming Down." Rainwater raised his eyebrows. It was an interesting choice for a funeral. It made him wonder anew about what kind of man Joe might have been. If anyone else thought it an odd choice, they didn't seem to respond. The pace was slower than Rainwater was expecting the song to be, perhaps in deference to the occasion, but it sounded good. When the trio finished the song, a smattering of nervous applause came forth, as if people weren't certain they should clap at a funeral. Jim paid no attention to the applause, but tuned his guitar, although if it was out of tune, Rainwater certainly hadn't noticed. Rainwater mused about the music. What songs would he choose for his service? What kind of service would he even have if he died? He set his lips firmly. Who would even miss Rainwater if he died? If he fell asleep under an oak and never awoke, who would ever look for him? It wouldn't be the worse way to go, he supposed, but did he hope someone would miss him? It was a part of the choice he had made, he supposed. Resting under an oak for eternity would be fine, and perhaps people who would miss him had already done so. Then, he could imagine many other outcomes as his final resting place, outcomes far less tranquil than under a tree. He found himself staring at the ground between his folded legs. Would tree fertilizing be Rainwater's purpose? Was that it?

Rainwater's attention was refocused on the ceremony when a young woman in a black pants suit came and stood next to Jim and spoke something low, unintelligible, but amplified across the little valley. Then she and Jim sang "Go Rest High on that Mountain," the young woman's voice quaking at the end. Her notes were clear though. When they finished, no one clapped, and the woman leaned over the microphone and said softly, "Bye, Daddy." Rainwater felt a knot in his throat. The young woman walked away quickly and preacher came back to the microphone.

"Joe was one of our newer members to our church family, but he was welcome, as are all of God's children. There are many rooms in His house." It seemed he glanced up toward Rainwater, but Rainwater couldn't be sure. He felt suddenly conspicuous. Perhaps he should leave. But no one else turned or took note, so maybe it was just Rainwater's imagination. Two crows flew across the small valley just over the metal roof of the shelter and Rainwater traced their path across the sky. They landed in a large pecan tree on Rainwater's side of the lane. The minister continued. "We want everyone to stay and listen to the music, to exalt in God's glory, and, we just pray, to be a little bit closer to God today. We are one in God's sight. Please know you are welcome. And we've got dinner up at the church when we are done. Please come and dine with us as we celebrate the church's victory with the family. One of the things Joe loved about our church family was when we all came together . . ." Another loud strum of the guitar cut him off, and this time the minister just smiled and moved away from the microphone. The guests chuckled approvingly. Another man who had been standing to the side with an electric guitar stepped forward now. He wore a fringed jacket, big cowboy boots, and a black Stetson. He leaned toward the microphone familiarly.

"Thank you, brother." He gave a tip of his hat to the minister who stood to the side, his Bible in both hands before him. "I want you to know, Reverend, I'm just glad this event is being held outdoors, 'cause brother, I ain't seen the inside of a church in twenty-five years and heaven only knows what might happen if I went inside yours." He nodded towards the minister and everyone gave a laugh. "Joe was the finest guitar player I ever played with. He could make an angel weep on those strings. Joe and I, we played a lot of gigs together through the years, we might've even seen some of you there, but don't worry: I won't tell on you." People laughed again. "This here was one of our favorites." He turned, bobbed his head once, and began playing a loud rendition of "The Dirt Road." The beat was catchy and Rainwater found himself tapping his foot sideways into the ground. The attendees nodded to the beat as well. The man with the Stetson was obviously a professional. He played several songs, after which people clapped, then he stepped aside and left the microphone to Jim. Jim played a few more songs and some church members stood at the microphone and gave an uneven version of "The Old Rugged Cross." Another older woman came and sat at the electric piano and played "I'll Fly Away," although she seemed sometimes ill at ease with the electric keyboard, hitting extra notes in the middle of some of the musical sentences. Rainwater sat back in the sunlight that had now reached him, soaking in the warmth and the music. He felt privileged to enjoy this celebration but it also gave him pause to reflect. Truth was, he didn't even know where he was heading, much less what his purpose might be. If Rainwater was a man of the road, shouldn't he at least know to what town he was heading, what he might do when he got there, besides walking in sand? Or maybe that was enough. Maybe being aimless was the entire point after all. At the end of the service, there were maybe a dozen singers standing behind Joe's coffin. They clapped and swayed and sang, "Will the Circle Be Unbroken." The audience also clapped and joined in once the singers waved them to. The minister came forth again, invited everyone to stay to eat, then blessed all in attendance. Rainwater decided it might have been the best memorial service he had ever attended, although he could not recall many beyond elderly relatives who had passed on when he was a child. He wondered suddenly if he had missed some since he had left. No doubt he had. He felt a sudden pang. Who?

The attendees now ambled up the incline towards the church and the parking lot and the cars strewn along the side of the country road for several hundred feet in either direction. For the most part, people kept their heads lowered, solemn still, although a few called out to acquaintances across the clearing, waving and smiling. The woman who had been sitting in the front row, Becky, stood, greeted a few well-wishers, then began walking away from the casket. She stopped, turned around, and went to stand at the head of the box, next to a spray of roses. She put her hand on the coffin and stood for several minutes, then stepped away again. As she did, she looked up, and it seemed her gaze rested on Rainwater again. Although he couldn't imagine anything he might have done wrong, Rainwater never knew how folks would take things. Besides, funerals are very personal things. Becky started making her way towards the church, talking with people along the way. Rainwater started gathering his packs so he could leave, but his leaning against them had pushed the top open on one so that half the contents spilled onto the grass where he was sitting when he went to sling it across his back. Rainwater hurriedly began repacking the bag, stuffing his items in more disheveled than he liked them. One of the crows called loudly above him and he started just a moment, looked up, then renewed his packing.

"Were you a friend of Joe's?" The voice behind him surprised him. He spun and saw Becky standing with the man in the black suit, his gaze turned down and a deep frown painted across his face. His focus seemed somewhere far away. He looked up at Rainwater when Becky spoke to him, but his expression did not change.

"Uh, well, no, I didn't, Ma'am." Rainwater lowered his gaze too. "I just happened by, heard the music, and thought I would listen a bit. Hope that wasn't too presumptuous of me." Rainwater cinched up his now full pack.

Becky managed a small smile. "No, that's fine. In fact, I think my brother would have loved that you stopped. Joe always said, music cures what ails you. Joe's music always made everyone feel better." She paused. "I can't believe he's gone." Her gaze now was unfocused as well. She returned her attention to Rainwater. "You're new around here, aren't you?" It was less question than statement.

"No ma'am. I mean, I'm not at all 'around here,' at least in the way you mean it. I'm just passing through, trying to decide which road to take, and heading on my way." Rainwater swung his pack onto his shoulder. The man beside Becky still did not speak.

"Oh." She looked away again. Rainwater was not sure she was listening, but it didn't matter. Then she looked back at Rainwater. "There are a hundred casseroles up here in the church. Won't you come join us?" She managed another wan smile. The man behind her looked up at her, expressionless now.

"Oh. No. Thank you. I'm fine." Rainwater could not see himself being so bold as to go into the church to eat with these mourners. He rarely turned down food and at the moment, he had no idea when or where he would eat again, but that was the trail he had chosen. It was not in his path to horn in on these grieving family members.

"There's plenty. And Joe would have wanted it."

"No, Ma'am. Thank you. From what I heard today, I think your brother was evidently a great man, but I can't do that. That just wouldn't be right."

"Hmm," Becky bit her lip. "Yeah, you know, Joe really was a great man, in his way. I'm afraid some folks might've thought otherwise, but to me, he was a great man. He made mistakes. We all do. And he's gone too soon. But he was a great brother. A great musician. A great friend. A great," she caught her breath up sharply, ". . . a great man." A tear wriggled its way down her cheek and she brushed it away. "Thank you for that. Yes, my brother Joe was a great man, in his own way, in a way he defined for himself. I want to remember him always as a great man." She reached over and patted Rainwater's arm slightly, gave a bittersweet smile, then turned away and retreated towards the church. The man with her stood still for a moment, watching her walk away, then turned his head to look back at Rainwater.

"Wait a minute?" the man asked.

Rainwater wasn't sure what he wanted but he nodded his assent. Rainwater had no place he needed to go especially, and no time frame for not getting anywhere. The man followed Becky to the little red brick church. Rainwater heard a motor behind him, turned and watched as a long silver and white hearse pulled down the valley and made its way to the coffin. Four men got out and started loading the casket into the car. They quickly moved the flowers out of the way, grabbed the corners and slid the casket into the hearse in a smooth, practiced motion. Rainwater let his eyes survey the cemetery but he didn't see any fresh digging. But he couldn't see the entire cemetery, so maybe it was simply out of sight. Or maybe he was being buried someplace else. Maybe he didn't belong in that graveyard.

"Here." The man in the black suit handed a plastic shopping bag stuffed full to Rainwater. "A man's gotta eat." Rainwater could smell fried chicken and something spicy as well. He opened the top to look in. "Nothing mayonnaise. It'll keep."

"Uh, wow. Thanks." Rainwater looked from the bag towards the man. "Thank you so much."

"You're welcome. Thank you for coming." Rainwater thought that odd since he was there quite by accident. "And thank you for what you told my wife. Not enough people say good things about Joe. She needed that." His frown was gone for just a moment as he pressed his lips together firmly. "I hope you find your way, sir." He turned and walked away towards the church. Rainwater watched him walk away, digesting his last comment for a few moments. He hiked his packs farther up his shoulder and started back up Elkhorn Tavern Road.

Called Home

Everywhere I've been, it seemed like I was just passing through. From the moment I left home and joined the merchant marines, looks like I never can find a branch to light upon long enough to make a nest. Make no mistake, it's what I chose. And sometimes, I like it like that. Nothing to tie me down. No bills. No responsibilities. Then, I've missed a lot too. Yeah, I've missed a lot.

Rainwater had camped for four days in a clearing in the woods that spread up a small hillside next to the truck stop. He had taken the time to set up a bit of a campsite beyond merely putting up the small dome tent he had received as a gift some weeks before. He had cleared away the twigs and rocks where he had set the tent. He tied to a tree a plastic shopping bag picked up along the road to use for trash. He had gathered wood in varying sizes to use for a campfire each night after dark when he seemed to be alone, although the backdrop of rumbling diesel engines reminded him he was not far from the rest of the world. Inside his tent, he unrolled the sleeping bag and made a pillow out of some of his clothes stuffed into a new sweatshirt he had received from the doctor and his sons in Simonton. His remaining items he had removed from his pack and lined up neatly along one side of his tent. In its own way, Rainwater had made the tent into more of a home than he had had in a long time, since he had left Ohio, perhaps.

He had a tiny flashlight that he had found in his gifts that gave out a meager yellow light, but was at least enough to read by in his tent late. He picked up pieces of a newspaper blowing around the truck stop parking lot, intending to use them to start his fire, but decided reading them first would give him some pleasure and have the papers serve multiple purposes. It was a local paper from the small town nearby, with stories mostly about local events. There was a rift that was evidently building between two of the local towns, with one mayor accusing the city leaders in the other of trying to steal away a local merchant. There were pictures of people just getting married and those celebrating many years of marriage. The county baseball team had a middling record, with one page of the paper carrying photos of every player in various poses, holding a bat in a make-believe batting stance, although with no helmet and grinning broadly, or reaching up with a glove to catch a nonexistent baseball, again with a big smile. They were handsome boys, by and large, and looked very young to Rainwater. It caused him to wonder if his grandchildren played sports, if he had any grandchildren. Or maybe they were gone away to school now. Just how old would they be? Rainwater added up the years in his head and the results meant he had probably missed it all. Had it been worth it? Had he protected them at all, or simply hurt them? Rainwater tried to shake off the doubt. He told himself he might just show up at a local baseball game and watch the kids play. Maybe that would make him feel less alone, less desolate. But then he realized from the article that the season had finished. Of course. It was high school and according to the newspaper, it was June 1. Whatever season the local team had had did not extend this late, perhaps due to losing too many games.

It was feeling like June, warm in the day, making the tent too warm to stay in during the daylight, but cool enough at night for Rainwater to sleep comfortably after sitting on a big log he had dragged over to his campfire, and watching the flames inexorably devour the twigs and branches Rainwater poked into the fire. He kept one stout limb as his reusable fire-stirring stick, shoving the flaming logs around to allow air through. For each of the four days, Rainwater had set about gathering firewood after meting out to himself the last remnants of vinegary coleslaw and white dinner rolls he had kept from the food he had been given. Rainwater had walked and hitched his way north along the US highway and now found himself along the Andrew Jackson Highway outside a town called Whitman. Rainwater had picked up a ride in Georgia with a trucker hauling lawn mower engines, but the trucker was heading east from there. Rainwater was heading north. Rainwater was heading home.

It was after he had stumbled upon the funeral service for a man he had never known, a musician named Joe, that Rainwater decided it was time. And having decided, he felt settled, as if some hole somewhere within him was suddenly filled. He had hiked, his thumb raised over his shoulder, for miles, until he turned the corner of the US highway. He didn't expect a ride from the mourners, or from local drivers for that matter on the small rural roads he had found himself on. But once he reached the highway, he had turned around and faced the traffic, holding his thumb up and trying to implore with his stance, his face, his eyes: Please give me a ride home. A trucker had picked him up and bent his ear about the trucker's son, about his wife who was waiting for him in North Carolina, about his dog, and even about the farm they wanted to buy someday. It was different. Usually, people wanted to hear about Rainwater and his travels, a fact that Rainwater had felt was vaguely intrusive but meager payment in the end. After his ride up to Carolina with the lawn mower trucker, however, he realized he missed it when the man seemed utterly disinterested in Rainwater's life. He had only wanted someone that he could tell about his own life. But Rainwater certainly couldn't be upset with the man. He had given him a ride, after all. And he had let Rainwater use his shower credit when he fueled up, and that was very generous.

In fact, Rainwater had done a great deal of cleaning up. He had trimmed his white hair again, still shaggy but shorter. There was only so much he could accomplish with his pocket knife. He had cleaned and trimmed his nails with the same tool, and had managed to scrape off his beard with a disposable razor he had plucked from the trash can in the shower room. In the cloudy mirror of the washroom, Rainwater tried to assess just how presentable he was. He looked tired. He looked older than he felt, although he felt pretty old too, but he looked like he was ninety, what with the weight loss and the wrinkles across his face from squinting so much in the sunlight. But it didn't matter. He was who he was. It would have to do. And now, back at his tent, Rainwater was packing up to head out. It was early morning and the tent still had dew on it. He went into the tent and rolled up his sleeping bag and stuffed it far down into his pack. He started putting together his clothes, but stopped when he picked up a faded brown tee shirt he had had for longer than he could remember. It was faded and stretched out along the bottom and the neck was unraveling as well. He placed it aside and went through the rest of his clothes, sorting out the ones that were worn out and falling apart. He put in the throw away pile the small, tattered blanket he had kept for so many years. Holey socks, stained kerchiefs, worn out pants – they all went into the same pile. When he had stuffed the rest into his pack, it felt lighter, but Rainwater wasn't sure if it was because the items he took out had added weight. There was little of substance left to weigh much. No, maybe it was leaving behind the need for them. Maybe it felt lighter because he felt stronger. Rainwater cinched up his pack and took down his tent, storing it in the other pack he carried. Then he scattered the gathering of branches and logs he had gathered together for his campsite. He wanted it to look as if he had never been there. He took the trash bag down and tied it together with the old blanket, slung the packs on the shoulders, and walked over the small rise to the truck stop to meet up with the trucker he had met earlier who was going to Cincinnati. Rainwater felt a bounce in his step as he walked over to the trash bin and threw away the old clothes and trash. He walked over to the parking area where the trucker with his load of batteries was ready to head off to Ohio. Rainwater almost wanted to run over, as if shackles had been removed from his ankles. Rainwater climbed up the passenger side of the cab and slid his packs behind the seat. He had not eaten and not drunk anything, because he knew they wouldn't stop for a long time. Besides, he had nothing to eat and nothing to buy any food with. The early morning cool air smelled of burning diesel. When the driver, whose name was Malcolm Rainwater had learned, climbed into the driver's side from his precheck of the trailer, Rainwater sat in the seat, buckled in, his hands folded, feeling every bit like he was ten years old and heading on vacation. Malcolm glanced over at Rainwater.

"Ready?"

"Yes sir."

Malcolm shifted the gears and pulled the big rig out across the parking lot and onto the highway. Once they were out on the road and Malcolm had finished shifting, he took a sidelong glance again at Rainwater.

"So, Cincinnati, huh?"

"Yes sir." Rainwater still sat stiff, straight-backed, looking forward, his hands crossed in his lap. Sister Mary back in school would have been proud, he decided.

"Why?"

Rainwater looked over now. "What?"

"Why Cincy? There's a million towns to go to, why Cincy?"

"Oh." Rainwater looked through the windshield again. "It's home." He paused. "Maybe." Malcolm gave a nod.

"It's time, I guess. I've got family there, I think. I hope. And besides, I have some unfinished business there, too."

"Business?" Malcolm asked it as if Rainwater having any sort of business dealings was absurd. The truck rumbled towards Lumberton. Malcolm gave Rainwater a quick once over.

"Yeah." Rainwater bristled at the notion just a bit. "I got business." He paused. "Well, police business, really." Malcolm gave a quick glance. He was twice the size of Rainwater, so Rainwater knew he did not feel threatened by this confession. "I need to go back and face up to something I've done. There comes a time when a man has to own up to his past, whatever that is." He paused again, not wanting to sound as if he were accusing Malcolm of anything. "We all have things we maybe aren't so proud of. I've got mine. I have to pay for what I did." Rainwater struggled with where this was going, but if was going to own it, he would have to be able to say it eventually. Only then could he try to find his family, although that would maybe have to wait until he did his time, whatever that would be. But he would do the time. He would do what he had to do now.

"Huh. Really?" Malcolm kept looking from the road to Rainwater and back, as if trying to size up this skinny old man and, perhaps, wondering if he had given a ride to the wrong man. "So, what? You turning yourself in?"

"Yep."

"Huh." He glanced again. "So, what did you do?"

"I killed my best friend." The truck swerved just a tad as Malcolm sat up suddenly and gripped the steering wheel tightly with both hands. Rainwater felt the rush of emotion as he said it aloud for the first time ever. He had never, ever told anyone about the incident, and now, saying it, it all became instantly very real. He fought back tears. "I'm sorry? You killed your friend? Why? How? Wait . . ." Malcolm looked back and forth from the road to Rainwater.

"I didn't murder him or anything, but I killed him just the same. I killed him," Rainwater almost yelled. Then he buried his face into his hands. "I killed him by being stupid.

He was my best friend. Hell, my only friend, really. And I killed him. I was stubborn and scared and stupid and I killed him. I wouldn't listen. He told me, but I wouldn't listen. I was afraid I'd lose my job and I refused to listen. He told me it was broken but I wouldn't stop. I sent him out on the floor and the goddamned thing broke and killed him. And it's all my fault." Rainwater drew in his breath and heard a sob come from his chest and it felt overwhelming. He stopped talking, breathed deeply, gathered himself, and said quickly, "It was at work. An accident that I caused that killed my best friend Don." Rainwater looked out the side window.

"Oh." Malcolm grew quiet and neither of them spoke for several miles. Rainwater faced out the window, but he was seeing the crash, seeing his friend's body pinned beneath the crates, seeing the whirl of confusion that ensued. The U.S highway outside the truck had become an interstate. The truck rumbled on and Rainwater felt himself suddenly removed from it all. He had made up his mind to return and face whatever charges there would be. And now he had told someone what happened. He had confessed, if only to an acquaintance. As difficult as it had been to say it, it was as if he had removed a chain tied tightly around his chest. His mind still felt a little dizzy from the emotion of it all, but he also felt relieved of a heavy load. He let himself sigh several deep breaths, calming himself, and then he felt sleep coming over him so he leaned against the window and slept.

When Rainwater awoke, he saw the road sign announcing that they were nearing Rockingham. He rubbed his eyes. "Oh. Wow. How long did I sleep?"

"I dunno. An hour maybe. You okay?"

"Yeah. Thanks. Sorry to spring that on you" Rainwater dropped his gaze towards the floor. "I've been running for a long time. I guess I just needed to get that off my chest."

"Yeah, well, that's a big one." Malcolm was leaning familiarly against the door of the cab as he drove. "So, I've been thinking. You said it was an accident at work. If it was an accident, it's not your fault, is it?"

"No, sir. It was my fault. I was the one that sent him out. I did it. And I need to pay for it."

"Huh," Malcolm huffed.

The truck wheels whining gave a constant backdrop, but the two men fell silent, Malcolm leaning against the door and Rainwater watching the trees pass along the side of the road. Finally, Malcolm leaned towards the dash and asked "Music?" at the same time he turned on the stereo.

"Sure." Rainwater shrugged.

"Who you like?" Malcolm twisted one of the dials. There were so many dials and buttons and gauges, Rainwater couldn't imagine how he knew what each one did.

"Oh, well. I don't know. I don't really know who's playing much. Anything's fine.

"Country it is then." The door next to Rainwater vibrated with a deep bass and a man started singing. Rainwater settled in to listen. The sound was good, but the words were quite sad, and Rainwater found listening to the singer tell about a love that had been lost, and then sing about missing home, and then croon a love song made Rainwater feel sad and pensive. But it was better than counting the miles down by following the mile markers so he just listened and tried to think of something else. He tried to imagine what his daughters might be doing on a warm summer day. After a bit, the man on the sound system stopped singing and a woman began, and she sang a song about dancing and honky tonks. Rainwater liked her voice and music was more upbeat. Maybe his daughters took vacations in the summer. He had taken them on a few, when they could scrape together funds, and they usually camped when they went to save on travel expenses, but everyone had fun. He hoped the girls had had fun. He pictured them in their pony tails, hopping around a campground, chasing each other. Long, bending notes played now on the stereo and the woman singing started off with a slow, "Oooo," before Malcolm reached over and flipped a switch and the cab returned to the same backdrop of the big tires moaning underneath them.

"Never liked that song," Malcolm resumed his lean against the door. A road sign flashed by announcing they were approaching High Point. They rode in silence a few minutes. Rainwater could tell Malcolm was running an idea in his head by the way he nodded absently as he drove.

Finally, the driver leaned towards Rainwater and said, "So, you said Cincy is your home?"

"Yeah, I grew up there. That's the last place I guess I ever really called home."

"So, you think you have family there still?"

"Well, yeah. Maybe. I had a wife there, but she's probably moved on. Or…" Rainwater pushed the idea away. "I had children there. Daughters. I don't really know if they still are. They'd be grown now, so who knows?"

"Yeah, I've thinking about that." Malcolm nodded. "You know, I have a computer in that bag behind your seat. We could do a search for them. Maybe see if you can find them? You could maybe even call them. You can call them on my cell." He looked over at Rainwater.

Rainwater considered it. He could maybe find them, but if he had to go to prison, would his calling be an even crueler act? "I don't know. I have to see what there is I have to do. I might need to wait until I find out if I am going to jail."

He hated saying it, it sounded entirely plausible, but he also wanted to confront the real possibility.

"Uh huh. I've been thinking about that too. Now, I don't know much about law, but if your buddy died in an accident, that means it wasn't like you meant to do it or anything."

"No, that's true. No, I never would've hurt Don. He was like a little brother to me."

"Okay, so that would mean it's not like you committed murder or something, right?"

"Yeah, I guess." Rainwater felt a bit uneasy with the path this conversation seemed to be on. He had accepted confessing, but talking about the details seemed inappropriate, somehow.

"So, that would not be murder, it would be, maybe something like manslaughter, and, even if they did say it was your fault, something like that might have a statute of limitations, or something. It would be maybe something like 20 years or so. How long you been gone anyway?"

Rainwater had not thought that deliberately about the legalities of the event. In fact, when he did think about those events, which was often enough, it was to see the scene of Don dead on the concrete floor of the warehouse. The word "slaughter" made him cringe on the inside. "Huh. I don't know. Longer than that maybe. But it doesn't matter. I have to find out. I need to know. And I want to pay for what I did to my friend."

"Well, my friend, you're gonna need a good lawyer. Maybe your daughters could help you find one. You really should call them, you know."

Rainwater could not imagine asking his daughters for anything. "Truth is, Malcolm. I don't even know their last names now or anything about where they might be. No." Rainwater shook his head. "No, I'm going to need to wait on that"

He shook his head again. "Thanks. I appreciate it, but I have to see what lies in my own road before I take that turn." Malcolm looked over and shrugged. Rainwater reached into his pants pocket and pulled out a small, thin sheeted new testament and started reading. It was a manner he used often before to stop unwanted conversations. The road rumbled beneath them. For a while, both men fell silent.

"So, you're a religious fellow, huh?"

Rainwater put the book down now in his lap. He was tired of using the same ruses to get the same results. It made little sense to decide to stop living this lifestyle and then revert to it at the first opportunity. He put the small book back in his pocket

"No, I'm not really. I was given that book by a couple of fellows in West End Park. They just walked up and handed it to me and I took it, of course. They were handing them out to everyone. When you have nothing, anything is wealth. Besides, it was small and easy to carry. It was something to read. I can quote you chapter and verse, but to be honest, I'm not sure what I believe any more." He looked out the window again. He did not want to read now. He wanted to finally settle this whole thing, and the more he thought about it, the more anxious he felt about it all. He watched a highway sign approaching. They were almost to Winston-Salem.

"Well, me and the missus, we go to the Methodist church. Her granddaddy was a preacher so her papa took religion pretty serious. Connie's not as serious about it as her Papa, but we still go. We always wanted the kids to have an upbringing where they could decide for themselves. Now, they're all grown up and taking the grandkids to a Baptist church. Can you imagine that? Baptists. Both of them. Never thought I'd see my kids being Baptists, but that's what they are. But it works for them. I don't say anything. It's none of my business. Like I said, we wanted them to choose. We just didn't want them to choose Baptists." He gave a laugh. "My oldest, Van, he's an engineer over in Wilmington. Works with fiber optics. Smart kid. Takes after his momma!" He snorted another laugh. Rainwater listened in silence. "He and Joanie have two girls and we just love them to pieces. Maggie and Vivian. Pretty girls, and smart as whips. Yeah, there's nothing like grandkids." Malcolm trailed off. He gave a sidelong glance at Rainwater. "Um, yeah, sorry if I . . ."

"So, you said both of your kids. Where's the other one?"

Malcolm brightened again. "Oh, Becca! Well, we call her 'Becca.' But her real name is Rebecca Jane, after Connie's great aunt. She married a fellow she met over at the university, nice kid, named David. They live over in Fayetteville. Got two boys, Rex and JoJo. We see them a lot too. Sweet boys. We divide the trips between the two kids, and of course they come home to Gramma's and Grandpa's for the holidays and all." Malcolm stopped talking suddenly, as if he remembered something. "Hey, I didn't mean to bend your ear about family and all. Didn't really think about how, you know, . . ."

"No, not at all." Rainwater raised his hand in a stop motion. "I like hearing about them. Matter of fact, it gives me hope that maybe I'm going to have some stories one day." Rainwater gave a thin smile at Malcolm, who nodded but drove on in silence until they reached Wytheville.

"You doing okay?" Malcolm looked over at Rainwater.

"Yes sir. I'm good." The road grumbled under the tires. Soon they were in West Virginia, a state Rainwater had not seen much of, his paths taking him along the coast, usually, or along backroads in the south and Midwest. He felt at home along the sea, and in the Midwest where he had lived. Rainwater watched the mountain scenery pass, deep ravines interspersed with high rounded mountains. And trees. There were lots of trees everywhere. Rainwater watched out the window for a long time.

Rainwater twisted around in his seat to face Malcom. "I grew up in the Church of Christ. Not the one that doesn't like the windows and statues, the other one. My mom and dad took us pretty much every Sunday. I liked it there. Had some friends. Knew the people who sat around us. Funny, it's not like we had to sit in one spot, but we did, and everybody else did too, mostly, so we knew Mrs. Underwood, who sat behind us. She sang every song like she was singing at the Met. Big voice. Me and my brother called her Mrs. Underwear under our breaths. Thought we were so funny. We'd started calling her that early on and one of us would say it and get the other giggling and Dad would give us a look, but you know how giggles are: once you start, they take on a life of their own. So we'd giggle and Dad would give us a look and then Mom would give us a look that was supposed to mean something like, 'I'm going to beat you,' but we knew we were safe. She wasn't likely to wail on us at church. So one of us would say 'Mrs. Underwear' to the other again and we'd get the giggles all over again. We did that just about every Sunday. After a while, we didn't even have to say the name. We'd just look at each other and know what the other was thinking and we'd start up giggling. Dad thought we were nuts. We hadn't even said anything, so he couldn't imagine what it was we were so silly about." Rainwater paused. He looked through the windshield at the billows of white clouds that reached from somewhere beyond the horizon. "I wonder where Sam is now. I wonder if Sam . . .."

Malcolm looked over at Rainwater.

"That your brother? Sam?"

"Yeah." Rainwater broke from his reverie. He glanced across the truck cab. "Yeah. I have a lot of catching up to do." He looked down at his hands in his lap and spent a long time thinking about his brother and the things they had done before, when they were kids, and even later, when they were both working but in cities far enough away they didn't get to visit as much except for the phone calls that had eventually tapered off from lack of effort. Rainwater wanted to call Sam right now, but he still had to take care of his business first. He still needed to confess his crime to the police. Then, maybe, he could call his brother. Yeah, he could call Sam and tell him he was still alive and sorry he had not been a better brother, sorry he had let so many years slip by. He would be able to tell Sam that his brother James was going to be a better man now. That was, of course, if he could find Sam, or if Sam were even still alive. Rainwater took a sharp breath at the thought.

"You okay?" Malcolm looked over at him.

"Yeah. I'm good." Rainwater fell quiet and watched the mountains pass again until they reached Charleston. After Charleston, the traffic intensified and Rainwater watched the cars and the other big trucks rolling through the passes, winding through the mountain passes on the big road. He noticed some of the license plates, from Maryland, Virginia, Kentucky. He remembered playing the state license plate game with his daughters when they had taken road trips, seeing who could find the most states. He recalled their playing the alphabet game as well when he saw an antenna atop a mountain. Where was the "B" word? There was a Buick. When they passed through Huntington, Rainwater looked down at the houses and businesses as they whizzed by. He felt anxious. When they passed the sign welcoming them to Kentucky, Rainwater recognized a nervous tickle in his stomach. Kentucky. The next state was Ohio and Cincinnati just there on the border. It wouldn't be long. Rainwater felt the need to use the toilet, but he held it without speaking. He had been with enough truckers to know they would take a break soon. They had to. It had been nearly eight hours. An oil refinery was on the left as they drove by, tall towers with spiraling ladders twirling up around them. A layer of steam and fog floated just above the lights and tanks. The eeriness of the plant made Rainwater uneasy. What would the authorities do to him? Where would they send him? Youngstown? No, maybe not. Maybe Lucasville. Rainwater glanced out his window, northward. Lucasville wasn't that far away from where they were right now. Rainwater shuddered. Maybe it was having to pee, he told himself. He decided he needed to divert his attention to the matter.

"I met my wife Carla when I was home on leave. I went to a dance up in Over-the-Rhine, where we weren't really supposed to go, and there she was, prettiest girl I ever saw. Her family had come over from Athens for her dad to find work and she was sitting there looking like she just stepped out of a magazine." Rainwater smiled now to recall it. "I never saw anything so beautiful in all my life, either before or since." Malcolm glanced over at him when he spoke. "I told my buddy she was going to be my girl before the night was out and he just laughed at me. I think he thought she was out of my league. And she really was . . . is . . .was." Rainwater waved his hand. "Maybe it was my uniform. That was why I wore it. Some girls like a fellow in uniform. Well, I asked her to dance and she said she would. Funny thing is, I really didn't know how to dance much, but she was so good, she made me feel like I was good. She was like a dancing dream out there." Rainwater looked away through the windshield. "Every other guy there was jealous of me, of me, James Rainwater, because she was dancing with me. Huh. Well, I was completely smitten. Never saw another girl in my whole life. When you find the right one, you just know." Rainwater let his mind's eye return to the dance. He danced with Carla over and over again in his thoughts. It made his throat tighten, but still he danced with Carla. Malcolm said nothing for a long time.

"Gotta stop." Malcolm was looking in his side mirrors. Rainwater jumped to hear the voice. He had been dancing with his wife, then courting, then having children, for what must have been hours. "Been eight hours. Besides, I gotta go." The exit sign said they were at Mt. Sterling. Malcolm used the compression release brake as he headed onto the exit ramp and the truck gave out a loud rapid fire ack-ack blast. Malcolm wheeled the rig into the service center and Rainwater nearly leaped from the cab as he brought it to a stop. He didn't realize just how badly he had to go until they started to stop. Rainwater was coming out of the restroom when Malcolm came in the door and met him halfway through the market area.

"We have to take thirty minutes. Settle in somewhere."

"Saw some picnic tables out here. Meet you there?"

"Sure." Malcolm started to walk away then turned around. "Hey, you want a hotdog or a bratwurst or something? My treat." He waved towards a machine that had various sausages turning on a roller grill.

"Thank you. Yes, please." Rainwater's mouth watered to think of food.

"They got a special. Any item and a soda. Help yourself. I'll be out directly." Malcolm turned and walked away. Rainwater picked the largest item he could find on the rollers, something called a hot link, and used the tongs to put it on a bun and then he added onions, relish, mustard, sauerkraut, jalapenos,

185

a tomato slice, and chopped lettuce. The bun was overflowing, but it was an easy way for Rainwater to get the most from his free meal. Malcolm walked behind him towards the roller grill. Rainwater stuffed the sandwich into a foil sleeve and poured a sugary soda from the machine. He didn't add ice. He wanted as many calories as he could get. He eyed the display of chips next to the grill area, wondering if he could talk Malcolm into a bag of chips as well, but decided he shouldn't risk asking too much. He was giving him a ride home, and buying him lunch. Rainwater reproached himself for even thinking of it. If he was going to give up being a fugitive and a beggar, now was as good a time as ever to start. While he attached the plastic lid to the drink, it occurred to him that maybe this was his last meal before prison. He stopped in his tracks for just a second to think of it. Regardless, that was the way it would have to be. Rainwater made his way over to the counter where Malcolm was already standing, his own drink and foil hotdog sleeve in hand.

Malcolm paid and they went out to the tables. It was breezy and pleasant outside, although the rumble of trucks pulling into the station kept it noisy. Rainwater sat at the table and looked over at the driver. "Thank you, sir, for my meal. Thank you very much." Rainwater tore open the foil sleeve and Malcolm's eyebrows raised.

"Now, by God, that's a sandwich." Malcolm laughed at the sight of all the condiments flopping onto the foil. Then he nodded and smiled. "You're welcome." Then they sat quietly and ate their sandwiches. Malcolm stood, threw away his trash, and walked over to his rig. He checked the tires, walking around the truck slowly, and he peered beneath the chassis of the trailer. Rainwater watched him follow what appeared to be a familiar pattern around the truck. Rainwater turned around and leaned against the table top and let the sun shine on his face. It felt warm and soothing and he felt calm and relaxed for a moment. He tried to let his mind wander back towards the dance hall, but it wouldn't come back, so instead he thought about Sandy and Sarah, his daughters, all grown up now, probably never even thought about Dad, not that he would blame them. After all that he had done. They would already know he was wanted, of course, for killing Don. And then he had run. Rainwater shook his head to think about the images they must carry. He wanted to make it up to them. He wanted somehow to make it all better, and the only way was to go and confess his crimes, do his time, and then, maybe, he could try, but not until then.

Malcom caught Rainwater's attention and motioned for him to come over. Rainwater gathered the trash from his lunch, sucked the last drop from the soda and tossed it all away. Rainwater climber back into the truck. The truck grumbled to life, hissed its air brakes and Malcolm pulled back onto the interstate highway. Outside the window, horse farms with rolling fields passed by. There were horses gathered in small groups in the green pastures. The hills were broken into geometric figures with black wooden fences. The blue of the sky made the green and black stand out. Rainwater had once thought he could live in Kentucky. He liked the farms and the horses, and, although he could scarcely recall the taste, his memory was that he had liked bourbon too. Rainwater watched the countryside roll past. When Malcolm took the turn north, Rainwater felt his stomach tighten. It would be happening soon enough. He stared out the window. Georgetown came and went.

"You want some music?" Malcolm reached towards the dash again.

"Actually, if it's all the same, I'd rather not."

"Okay, but it sure is quiet in here." Rainwater thought he heard tinge of admonishment in Malcolm's tone. Of course, Rainwater knew. One of the main reasons Malcolm had given him a ride was for some company on this long haul and Rainwater wasn't holding up his end of the bargain.

"So, back when I was a kid, me and my big brother Sam used to go fishing in this pond that was at one end of a golf course just outside of town. They called it Johnson's Lake, but it was really just a pond. We would ride our bikes out there, carrying our Zebcoes and little metal tackle boxes and a coffee can of sorry little worms we had dug up from the back yard. We would go out in the morning and stay all day, fishing. I loved it. It was a pretty good distance from where we lived but we didn't care. We wanted to go fishing. It didn't help that I was riding one of those little sting ray bicycles, so I had to pedal twice as many times as Sam did, since he had this big old Schwinn that he used to deliver newspapers. Well, it was a pretty busy road that went out there, and kind of twisty, so we were doing a lot of balancing and trying not to get run over at the same time. We were heading out one time, and Sam's tire hit a rut just as this woman in a station wagon was whipping past us. Sam fell right into the passenger side door of her car as she passed by. Then his bike slid under the back wheel and it went flying off the road and into the ditch. Well, the woman slammed on the brakes and jumped out of her car. I think she was half expecting to see Sam's bloody body smeared along Leitchfield Road, but he hopped up, gathered his fishing stuff and started down the embankment to get his bike. Well, the woman was freaking out. She waved down a car and had them go call an ambulance to check Sam out, but he was fine. He was mad because it seemed like he wasn't going to get to go fishing. He was really mad about that. Funny thing is, he didn't really have a scratch on him. His bike, it was ruined, but Sam was fine. They came and got him and made him go to the hospital and I didn't know what I was supposed to do after they had snatched him up, so I went on over to Johnson's Lake and went fishing. I must've caught twenty bluegill in about an hour and a half. Mostly little ones, but I used to keep them all, pretty much. Then my dad shows up in the pickup truck and he's looking like I have lost my mind to have gone on and gone fishing. We put my bike on top of Sam's mangled remnants of a bicycle and he tells me to get in and I say, 'What about my fish?' And he looks at my stringer of bluegill I'm holding and just shakes his head. 'Put them in the back,' he says, and we head home where Sam is sitting on the porch swing sulking. He sees my stringer of fish and gives me a drop-dead look, and then when Dad pulls his mangled Schwinn out of the back, Sam's jaw drops and he just stands there staring at what was once his pride and joy. I lorded that day over him for years." Rainwater gave a chuckle. "Dad fixed his bike up almost like new. He was good at fixing things. Guess maybe that's where I got it." A sign said they were passing the exit for Sadieville. Rainwater's stomach tensed again and he returned to looking out the window.

"Where's your brother now?" Malcolm's voice startled Rainwater just a little.

"Pittsburgh. I think." Rainwater wondered what Sam thought about his leaving, about his running away. "Last time I knew, anyway. It's been a while."

"Well, maybe once you get things squared away?" Malcolm shrugged.

"Yeah, Maybe." Rainwater paused. "Yeah, I hope so." Rainwater pulled up mental picture of Sam. The last time he had seen his brother, he had jet black hair and those piercing brown

eyes that always gave him away when he told a story. Rainwater
tried to think of another story to tell, but his head was beginning to feel a little confused. It was so much to consider. Every
exit sign reminded him that they were getting closer to his
home, to his moment of coming to terms with his past.

"So, 'Rainwater'?"

"Yes?" Rainwater turned in his seat to face Malcolm.

"Is that a native American name or a road name, you know,
like, 'Big Bob' or 'Tiny'?"

"Oh. Well, it's actually my last name. And my ancestors
came from Germany or someplace like that so it's not native
American. My whole name is James Allen Rainwater. I just
shortened it on the road because it sort of described who I
am . . . was. Heading downhill by the easiest route possible."
Rainwater shook his head and gave a small smile. "My family
called me 'Jim.' Well, that's not true. Sam always called me
'Jimbo,' even as grownups. I liked that. Made me feel like a
kid every time he said it."

"Well, okay, Jim."

"Call me 'Jimbo.' I'm going home."

"Okay, Jimbo." Malcolm gave him a look and they fell
silent, watching the road ahead, until they made a veer and
the Spence Bridge over the river came into view. Rainwater
felt his entire body stiffen. Malcolm kept glancing over at him,
so Rainwater's anxiety evidently showed. They rumbled over
the Ohio River. "So, where is it you want me to drop you off,
Rain . . . Jimbo?"

"Well, anywhere that's convenient for you to pull off. I'm
heading over to Central Avenue, but I can walk."

"I can get you there. Hang on." Malcolm geared the truck
down and exited the highway. The big rig twisted through the
downtown on streets that Rainwater had driven on, walked

on, shopped on, lived on. His head was swirling. His time had arrived. Then Malcolm stopped the truck in the middle of the busy street, looked over at Rainwater, and said, "Good luck, my friend." He stuck his hand out. Rainwater shook his hand at the same time he realized where they were. It was only a couple of blocks to the police station. He was here. Cars honked behind them and Rainwater shifted in his seat, unbuckling his seatbelt and fidgeting with the door. "Don't worry about them." Malcolm looked absently into the side mirrors. "They'll be fine." Then Malcolm reached into his back pocket and pulled his wallet out. Rainwater was opening the cab door. "Here."

"No. No. I can't take your money. You've done so much. Heck, you've been harboring a fugitive all day. You better get out of here. I've put you in danger." Rainwater was perched on the step now pulling out his packs.

"Well, since I was bringing you here to turn yourself in, I think I'm safe on that account." Malcolm gave Rainwater a grin. "Take it. It's not a lot, but you don't want them adding vagrancy to the charges do you?" He held the three twenties out farther and Rainwater took them.

"Thank you, Malcolm. For all of it."

"You got it, Jimbo." Malcolm nodded his head and shifted the truck into gear as Rainwater jumped off with his packs. "I hope it turns out like you hope." Then the truck growled out diesel fumes and headed down the street. Rainwater hiked his packs higher onto his back and headed for the police station on Ezzard Charles Drive.

The Meaning
That You Choose

Regrets? Well, sure. Who doesn't have regrets? I've got plenty of them. Sometimes I regret the things that happened to me and then, sometimes, I regret things I see happening around me, things I can't do anything about, to people I don't even know. Did I cause them? Most likely not, but I can still regret that they're happening. But the things I did wrong, the things I could've done better? Anyone who says they don't have those regrets is kidding themselves. Or maybe they're just selfish. There's that.

"Jimbo? You ready?" Don knocked on the door as he opened it. His attention was drawn to the spindly artificial Christmas tree over in the corner of the living room. A smattering of small boxes were littered beneath it, all carefully wrapped. "Hey! Merry Christmas!"

"Yeah, Merry Christmas yourself, Donnie." Jimbo's tone was sarcastic as he strode into the room through the archway that led to the dining area. Small pencil lines with dates were laddered up the lower portions of the wall of the small arch. A maple-colored wood dinette table was decorated with paper-plate place settings colored with crayons. Jimbo was carrying a pair of work boots and he sat heavily on the sagging wingback chair to put them on. Two little blonde-headed girls followed him into the small living room and darted across the room to hug Don.

"Merry Christmas, Uncle Donnie!" The girl who was wrapped around his right leg grinned up at him.

"Merry Christmas, Sarah."

"What about me?" The one on his left leg looked up at him.

"You too, Sandy." Don caressed the tops of their heads.

"Hi, Donnie," a woman's voice called from farther back in the house.

"Hey, Carla. Merry Christmas!"

"Merry Christmas! You girls come on now, we need to get ready for Sunday school. I hear the reverend has a big service today." But the girls continued to be wrapped around Donnie's legs. They looked up with pleading eyes.

"What'd you get me, Uncle Donnie."

"You girls go get ready for church, like your Momma said." Jimbo barked and he pulled on the boots and threaded the laces through the eyelets. The girls moped away for two steps, then took off at a gallop through the small bungalow.

"Kids all ready for Christmas I see." Don nodded towards the table.

"Yeah. Yeah. They'll learn to get over that, I suppose. 'Fraid I don't have much for them this year. Pitiful." Jimbo gave a nod towards the sparse Christmas tree with its spattering of boxes and bags. "I hate that we can't do more. They've been really good. Makes me feel terrible, like a failure. Gotten so I can't stand Christmas."

"What are you talking about? Looks like plenty, Jimbo." Don sat now on the corner of the divan and waved away Jimbo's lament. "Don't you worry about it. The kids have all they need and we'll have a great holiday. You'll see." Now he waved towards the tree. "Looks like Santa's been good to them, if you ask me. And look at them, happy as they can be. You're doing fine, Jimbo. You and Carla both."

Jimbo laughed an unhappy chuckle. "Yeah, well, it doesn't actually look like much under the tree, and even worse, we wrapped up the things like the apples and little bags of ribbon candy so it would look like more." He wrapped a lace around the top of his boot twice and tied a knot.

"But that is more, Jimbo. Hell, there's starving kids in India who'd love to have those things for Christmas."

Jimbo was finishing his second boot. He stood and grabbed a long raincoat coat that had been draped over the back of the chair and gave his friend an even look. "Well, I dunno, Donnie. Pretty sure those starving kids in India are more likely to be Hindu than Christian." He headed for the door, his coat clasped in his fist. "Bye, Carla. See you girls later," Jimbo called as walked out. Donnie stood to follow him.

"You're right. I never even thought about it. Hey, I guess that makes Santa's night easier, you know? I mean, think of all those kids who are Muslim or Hindu or whatever. Makes his rounds easier, I'd say." He gave a chuckle as he followed Jimbo out the door and pulled it shut just as Carla called a goodbye from back in the house. It was warm out, for Christmas day, and the sun was bright. Donnie squinted as he came out. "Dang, sure is spring-like out here."

"Sure enough." Jimbo was already to Don's ten-year-old Fairmont on the street. "Come on, Donnie. We're gonna be late." Jimbo climbed in the passenger seat.

Don trotted out to the driver's side of the car. "Hey, I waited for you to put on your shoes, Jimbo. Don't blame me if we're running late." He slid into the seat, started the car and drove off.

"Aw, I'm just giving you the business. We're fine, Donnie." Jimbo lit a cigarette and rolled down his window to vent the smoke. They reached the corner and took the turn onto the busy through street.

"Hey, what time should we come by later, Jimbo?"

"I don't know." Jimbo shrugged. "Carla and the girls will be home after church, so if Karen wanted to go over with little Petey after church, they could."

"Well, I know she wants to go by her Momma and Daddy's, so I'm thinking later."

"Well, I wouldn't blame you if you decided you wanted to go spend Christmas someplace else. Won't be much of a Christmas at the Rainwater house, I'm afraid."

"What are you talking about? We always spend Christmas with you guys."

"Well . . ."

"And I wouldn't want to be anywhere else. What's the matter with you, anyway?"

"What?" Jimbo shrugged.

"You pissed off at Christmas or something? When we were kids, back in the old neighborhood, you were the one who always said Christmas was the best holiday there was. Didn't you always say that?"

"I was a kid, Donnie. We both were."

"True. But you gave me one of the best Christmas presents I ever got. And we were just kids."

"What are you talking about?"

"Marshall Bridges, Eddie Kasko, Frank Robinson?"

"Oh, that baseball." Jimbo smirked. He took another draw off his cigarette.

"Yeah 'that baseball.' I still have it. I couldn't believe you gave that to me."

"Well, truth is, your family didn't have as much as we did and . . ."

"And you gave me the best present ever." Don grinned over at Jimbo. "You told me Christmas was the best holiday ever, and you gave me your signed baseball just to prove it."

Jimbo looked out the window. "Yeah, I guess I believed it back then."

"You believed it on that Christmas afternoon a couple years later when you and Frances McConnell were playing spin-the-bottle with only the two of you over in her playhouse, didn't you?"

"Huh! Frankie. Wonder whatever . . ."

"And how about when you came home on leave with all those presents for everyone from Taiwan or . . ."

"Manilla. They were from Manilla."

"Okay, Manilla. You brought back something for everyone, even my kid sister Darlene, as I remember it."

Yeah, well, I had more money and fewer responsibilities then, I guess." Jimbo scowled now. "What's your point, Don?"

"I just hate to see you so down on everything, and hard on yourself. You never give yourself a break."

197

"I'm just frustrated. Wish I could do more." Jimbo gave a sigh.

"It'll be all right, Jimbo. Wait and see. It might be skinny right now, but you and Carla, you're gonna be fine." Don gunned the car through a yellow light.

"Trying to get a ticket?" Jimbo glanced over at him.

"Judgment call. Run the yellow or lock it up in the intersection. I chose the safest option, your honor." Don smiled at his friend who said nothing. "What's really eating at you, anyway, Jim? I've never seen you so mad all the time? You mad 'cause we're working Christmas? It was our choice, wasn't it? We get double pay."

"Yeah, I'm fine." He tossed his cigarette through the open window and rolled it up. "There is something . . ." He stopped short.

"Well?"

"It's just that I heard the supervisor talking with Fred the other day. They're talking about layoffs." Donnie twisted his head towards Jim.

"What? When? Who they talking about . . .?"

"Just talk, right now. Might even go down to two shifts."

"What?"

"What he said. I don't know. Might just be to stir everyone up. They do that too, you know."

"Yeah. They do seem to like to screw with Christmas, don't they?" Don shook his head. "Man, hope they don't put me out. Karen does okay at the loan company, but we need both incomes."

"Aw, I think you'd be safe, Donnie. You've been there longer than a lot of these guys. It'd be by seniority, you know. Might have to change your hours or something, but you'd be safe."

"Yeah, maybe." Don seemed to calm down at the thought. He turned the sedan into a parking lot along the row of warehouses. Cars were pulling in at several locations. "And you've been there even longer, Jimbo, so you should be okay too, right?"

"Yeah, I suppose. I don't know about floor managers, but yeah, probably. Sure don't want to make any waves, though. My guess is they're looking for reasons to let people go right now so they don't have to lay as many people off, you know?"

"Yeah, I do." They climbed out of the car and walked across the parking lot towards a large metal door that was propped open. Don nudged Jim. "Like that door propped open. That's a violation, you know."

"Well, I ain't saying a thing."

"Me either." They walked in and waited in line to clock in.

The man in front of them turned around and nodded. "You see they traded half the team for Sanderson?" His eyebrows were raised in alarm.

Jim gave a sarcastic sniffle. "Yeah, and I think his best days are behind him. Crazy."

"Yeah, me too. They ought to let me run the Reds, I'd show 'em." The man gave a laugh and turned around to clock in.

Jim clocked in, then Don, and they took their coats to the row of metal lockers beyond the time clock. They headed for the loading dock. Jim went over to the manager's desk and went over the trucking list with the manager coming off duty, who quickly turned around and left when they were done. Don walked over to Jim after the other manager had left. "His house on fire or something?" He looked after the man who was trotting over to the clock now.

"Well, it is Christmas," Jim offered. Don raised his arms as if to say, "Of course." "You want to start with that load of furniture in four, Don?" Jim pointed towards a trailer that had been backed in next to the loading deck.

"Yeah, sure, Jimbo. What's the matter? You in a hurry too?"

"I want us both to look sharp, Donnie. These guys are always watching." Jim glanced around him suspiciously.

"Okay, boss man. I'm on it." Don walked in a mock slow-motion run over to a forklift and climbed aboard. He shot Jim a grin. Jim just shook his head. Don cranked up the machine and started pulling it towards the open trailer, then he stopped, lowered the lift up and down a couple of times, and drove it further, then stopped it again. He scowled at Jim, who was talking with another dock worker now, and waved for him to come over. Jim finished the assignment to the other worker and went over, looking around him to see if anyone was noticing the shift getting off a little slowly.

"What's the deal, Donnie? You trying to get us let go? Come on, let's get that truck unloaded."

"There's something screwy going on with this lift, Jimbo. It feels like there's maybe something in the mast that's slipping or something." Don raised the lift and it popped a notch as it rose. "See?"

"It looks like it may have a hitch in it, but it's fine. Go on ahead and empty that truck, Donnie. Boss is watching." Jimbo nodded towards the truck of wooden crates the lift was pointing towards but cut his eyes toward a mirrored set of windows in a room above the warehouse floor.

Don lowered the lift and it popped again as it went down, but then it moved smoothly. "I don't know, Jim. We got another lift I can use?" Don glanced around the open space that he was supposed to fill with crates of furniture, but there were no other lifts around. All along the row of bay doors, the voices of men calling out instructions and machines clanking echoed.

"They're all out, Donnie. Just unload the truck. It'll be fine. They have to inspect these things, you know. It's fine or they would've taken it off line." Jimbo kept eyeing the mirrored windows.

Donnie looked at Jimbo and shook his head. "Jim, it feels like it's messed up. I think we need to report it." Don turned off the forklift and started to climb off the seat.

"Shit, Don. Sit down." Jimbo held his hands in a stop. "I already don't have a Christmas worth showing up for for the girls. I didn't even get Carla anything at all. And now you're going to get me laid off because you don't want to unload a truck or something?"

"Oh, that's not fair, Jimbo, and you know it." Don cocked his head to one side. "I've done the work of two men the whole time I've been here, ever since you got me this job, and I've done the jobs nobody else would even do. Don't pull that on me, Jim."

"Well, then go unload that damned truck, Donnie," Jimbo hissed.

Donnie spun back around in his seat. "Fine. I'll unload the goddamned truck, Jimbo. But this ain't right, and you know it." He gritted his teeth as he nearly growled the last part, then started up the machine and drove towards the open truck. Jim watched him drive off, then he turned and walked towards the manager's desk to check the other charts. He tried to see if he could tell if there was any movement in the office above him by focusing on his peripheral vision, but he couldn't see anything. Now he kind of hoped they were watching him manage a reluctant employee so well, getting the job done. It might just be the thing that could get a man promoted, Jim decided. A promotion would fix so much. Wouldn't that be a great present to give Carla that night? Jim let his mind see a scene of telling Carla that he got a promotion and a raise and that they were going to be so much better off. Maybe he could even stop at a store somewhere and get some more presents for the twins. But then, he was riding with Donnie, so that might not work out. A huge popping sound suddenly echoed through the warehouse and when Jim spun to see what it was, he saw Donnie leap to his left, his arms before his face, and he heard Don scream as two huge crates fell on him, flattening him onto the concrete floor and sending his hard hat skittering out the opening of the dock next to the truck. The forklift was tipping over as well and Jim ran towards the scene. Before he could get there, the lift fell in a thunderous crash on top of the one crate that was still on top of Don, splintered wood flying in all directions. Jim felt nauseous and he ran towards the cloud of dust that was still settling outward. Men were screaming and the door from the supervisor's office flew open and two men were racing down the metal staircase, yelling something. Maybe they were yelling at Jim, but he couldn't tell what they might be saying. Maybe they were yelling at someone else. Jim reached the heap of wood and metal where somewhere underneath his best friend lay just as two other men arrived. The three of them started throwing shards of wood and pieces of upholstered couches, trying to reach Don. Then Jim realized he couldn't hear anything because he himself was screaming his friend's name over and over.

"Don? Don? Don?" Jim threw planks and the two other men were lifting off one of the forks from atop the pile. The forklift itself was still leaning against the heap, it's engine idling. Now there were lots of men scurrying around the site. Someone turned off the forklift and it was now leaned off the rubble. That was when Jim saw Don. His head lay still on the concrete, a rivulet of blood seeping towards the open dock. His body was still covered with the tattered remains of furniture and wooden crates. The men were pulling the debris off but all Jim could do now is stare at his best friend.

"Shit. He dead?" The supervisor was pushing his way into the gaggle of men, some of whom were feverishly pulling items off the pile, the others just gaping at the mangled body that was being revealed as they uncovered him. Then the entire group of men broke into mish-mash of conversations, as Jim heard it. He had just pulled of the leg of a burgundy-covered couch from atop his friend's arm.

"Lookit that. Shit, no way he survived that."

"Yeah, he's gotta be dead. You see that?"

"I saw the whole damn thing. Lift failed on him."

"Ya think?"

"Oh my god, what happened?"

"What's his family . . ."

" . . .Christmas . . ."

" . . no way he could live through . . ."

". . .Broken forklift . . ."

"Who was his manager . . .?"

" . . think it was Rainwater . . ."

" . . . gonna be big trouble . . ."

" . . . go through the check?"

Jim stood looking down at Don's very still body. He suddenly felt dizzy and ill.

"Okay, stand back." The supervisor used his arms as a shield to hold back the men. "Ambulance has been called. Stand back, let them do their jobs. Be here in a minute." He looked down at the smashed body and shook his head. Then he looked up at the men around him. "Matter of fact, why don't all of you go do your jobs, too, okay?" The men shuffled backwards, still gawking at Don, who lay very still, his arms and legs akimbo in angles that were clearly not normal for the human body. Jim stepped back too. He was looking at Don, but he was seeing Karen and Pete, their little boy. He was seeing Sarah and Sandy when he told them. What? What would he tell them? That it was an accident? Or that Daddy had killed Uncle Donnie? He had killed him by being scared and stubborn. And what would that mean for him, for James Rainwater? He was going to prison, probably. Killing his best friend was not the punishment; it was the crime. His daughters and Carla would see him go to jail, and every detail would be aired at the trial. How he had ignored his friend's concern. How he had sent him to his death by refusing to listen. He was a killer. On top of all his other failures, he was a killer. He had already been unable to provide much more than basic needs for his family. And now that too would be gone. Before they put him in jail, they would fire him, of course, and why not? He had failed miserably at his job. Jim turned now and walked towards the door. At the last minute, he detoured over to his locker, pulled out his tattered raincoat, and then went outside to smoke from the pack of cigarettes in the pocket. An ambulance arrived, the siren only adding to the whirl of sounds Jim was hearing. Inside, the supervisor was yelling now, yelling for him.

"Where the hell is Rainwater? Rainwater. You gotta come fill out the accident report." The supervisor was screaming, but the backdrop was of machines rumbling and engines running. Work was going on, although now no one was talking much. Jim considered it for a moment. There would be a report filed first, then the investigation, then the trial. Maybe not. He would just plead guilty. Why not? He was guilty, wasn't he? He was guilty of killing Donnie. He had killed Donnie. Jim leaned his head into his hands and sobbed deeply. He felt suddenly hot and tired, exhausted. He had to get away from the noise, from the supervisor yelling. He had to think about what he should do. He walked across the parking lot towards Don's car, but when he got there, he didn't try the door. He knew it was locked and that the key was on Don's dead body. Instead, he walked past the car towards the patch of brown grass that separated the parking lot from the street and the walking seemed to cool him down some, so he walked on down the street. He ran the picture through his head time and again. He couldn't change the outcome though. He was powerless to prevent what had happened, just as he had felt powerless to provide a decent home for his family, to feed them enough, sometimes. He thought about how the girls were only allowed a half glass of milk with their meals to stretch the budget some. It was pitiful, and now, worse. Much worse. He walked along the curb and walking away from the noise of the warehouse and the taste of the dust and coppery smell of Don's blood made it better, somehow. He just needed to think. But he could not escape that he knew he had destroyed two families that day, his own and Don's. Nothing would ever be the same. Ever. And Christmas – Christmas would forever be the awful anniversary of the day James Rainwater ruined so many lives. He would forever be the reminder of his failure as a man, as a human being. Maybe there was nothing he could do now but just go away and try to let everyone forget all about him. Maybe they would be able to heal if he were gone. Maybe they could make something positive of their lives if he wasn't there. It might be the only decent present he could give anyone since he gave Donnie his prized signed baseball. Rainwater walked to the end of the street where the through street led down towards the river. Rainwater turned the corner and worked his way towards the river.

Remembering the Future

There's not a road I go down, a bridge I cross, or a town I come into that I don't think about what might have been. When you travel alone, you have lots of time to ponder on things. That doesn't mean I always think how things might have been better. Sometimes maybe things could be better, sure, but lots of times, I think how things could've been even worse. Way worse. That makes me feel lucky. Now, to me, being lucky doesn't always mean you find a dollar on the street. Sometimes being lucky means that someone needed a job done and you were the one standing in front of them asking if they needed that job done. That's the kind of luck I like. You can have all the luck in the world that way.

James Rainwater walked slowly up Ezzard Charles Drive and stopped short in front of the grey and yellow building. He dropped his packs onto the sidewalk beside him. He looked up at the metal letters above the awning. This was it. He was there. Uniformed police walked in and out of the glass doors, sometimes talking with each other, sometimes looking at their phones, sometimes running. A few gave him a quick glance as they passed by but then they went about their business. He wondered how nonchalant they would be if they only knew they were passing by a fugitive; in fact, a killer and a fugitive. He picked up his bags and gathered his resolve. He had decided to turn himself in some days back, but going inside after all this time presented a new level of resistance within him. But he was tired of running. He was tired of looking over his shoulder constantly. He was tired of never knowing what would happen. Now, he knew what was going to happen. He was going to prison. But he deserved to be imprisoned. Hadn't he killed his best friend? Wasn't he the one responsible? No, he had to do this. He had to give Don's family some closure, even if it was so many years later. And his daughters deserved a finish to their years of neglect as well. They deserved better than James Rainwater. Maybe they too deserved to see him go to jail, to see him punished for running away so many years ago. He pulled open the glass door and entered the foyer. There were even more police inside. He felt his knees buckle just a little, but he kept walking until he stood before a battered desk that was turned to face the door he had come through. A uniformed policeman sat behind the desk, alternately flipping through some papers and looking at a computer screen.

"Yes, sir?" He stared at the computer screen for a moment and scowled. "Can I help you?" Now he looked at James Rainwater. He wondered what to do with his bags. What would they do with his meager belongings when they locked him up? The policeman was young, his hair cropped short. His face looked like a child's to James. James stood frozen in place. "Can I help you, sir?" The policeman's eyebrows were raised impatiently.

James tried to find words. He felt as though he had forgotten how to speak. But now the moment had arrived. "Yes." He croaked. His throat was suddenly very dry. He cleared his throat and tried again. "Yes, I'm here to turn myself in." The young policeman put down the papers he had been holding and stood now. He was much taller than James had thought from seeing him seated. The bags suddenly seemed very heavy. The officer looked over at another desk and nodded to someone, a knowing nod that seemed to speak more than words might have.

"Okay." The officer looked at James up and down, then he motioned to a chair next to James as the officer himself sat. "Have a seat." He kept his eyes on James, as if he was trying to remember something. No doubt he had seen his mugshot in his daily briefings, although they would be old now. How old had James been when he got in that fight, twenty-four? Maybe they had age progression technology and used that. He put his bags on the floor and sat tentatively on the chair. Sitting felt good. He hadn't realized just how shaky his legs had felt until he sat. He realized another officer was standing now beside him, this one a woman. She didn't speak so James stared ahead at the officer in the chair. "You have any identification?" The officer leaned forward on the desk, familiarly.

"Um, no. I haven't kept any." James looked down at his hands. They were rough, raw from too much cold and rain and wind. He paused a moment, trying to decide the best answer. "You don't keep identification when you're on the run. From the law." He said it evenly. It was easier, maybe, once he started.

If his answer surprised the officer in any way, he didn't show it. "Okay. Let's start with your name. Your last name?"

"Rainwater." He felt ashamed, suddenly. The officer scribbled on a piece of paper.

"First?"

"James. James Allen Rainwater, sir." He stared at his hands still. The officer clicked several buttons on the computer screen then keyed in the name. James felt a nervous nausea coming over him. He glanced at the officer next to him, a tall woman with a stern face. Rainwater wondered if he should maybe smile in greeting but such things seemed superfluous just now. The officer typing at the computer moved the mouse around, clicking, then reading, then clicking. He looked back at James without expression.

"Mr. Rainwater, what is it you are turning yourself in for, exactly?"

"I killed a man." The officer behind the desk shot a look at the woman beside James and she moved directly behind James so that James could no longer see her.

"Who? When?" The policeman picked up the pen again.

"His name was Donald Johnson." James paused. "He was my best friend." He felt his throat tighten. "It was a long time ago. But I killed him. On Christmas day, no less. Thirty years ago this Christmas. A bunch of shipping crates fell on him and it was my fault. I killed him."

The policeman looked surprised now. He typed on the computer again. "That's a long time to be on the run, Mr. Rainwater." He said it softly, as much to himself as to James, it seemed. "Where did this happen? Here in Cincinnati?" He looked confused as he scanned one screen then another. Now he talked to the officer behind James. "That's gonna be in the archives, isn't it? Or maybe cold case?"

"I'll check with Sergeant Wallace." Footsteps retreated from behind him.

"Yes, sir. Here in Cincinnati. It was down at Riverside Shipping, over on Matthews Road."

The officer cocked his head to one side as he read the computer screen. "Your name is James Allen Rainwater?"

"Yes, sir." James braced for it, the handcuffs, the search, the processing.

"How old are you, Mr. Rainwater?" He kept his eyes on the screen.

"Um, well, fifty-eight, sir." The policeman shot him a look, as if sizing up the veracity of his claim. "The road ages a man." The officer set his mouth firmly, then looked up at the female officer and the heavyset man walking up beside them. He stood now.

"What d'you got here, Klemper?" The heavyset man scowled at James.

"Umm, well, this is Mr. James Rainwater. He tells us he wants to turn himself in for killing his best friend, a Mr. Johnson, some thirty years ago, Sarge. Sounds like maybe an industrial accident?" He shook his head at the sergeant as he spoke and gave a shrug. "We don't have computer records from that far back." He signalled for the sergeant to follow him.

"Excuse us, Mister, what's the name? Rainwater? Rainwater. Sounds . . ." The sergeant and the officer stepped away. "Keep an eye on our guest, Franklin." The other officer put her hand on James shoulder. It seemed a bit of a restraint, but James took a sense of comfort from the touch nonetheless. The two men huddled several feet away, the younger one doing most of the talking. The sergeant bowed his head several times and gave a few "Uh huh" comments. He looked up now at Rainwater. "Really!"

"Yes, sir." Both of their voices grew just loud enough for James to hear.

"When was this? And where was this?"

The officer took the few steps back to his desk and picked up the piece of paper he had scribbled on and took it back to the sergeant. "He said Christmas day thirty years ago. Matthews Road. River . . ."

"Riverside Shipping." The sergeant finished the sentence and shot a sharp glance over at James. "Well, I'll be damned."

"Yeah, I don't know that place . . ."

"Went out of business right after that. I remember the incident. Was a rookie and got the Christmas duty." He walked away towards James, leaving the officer standing still for a moment, who then followed the sergeant. The sergeant sat at the desk and gave a quick signal to the officer gently holding James down. She removed her hand. "You can go, Franklin."

"Yes, sir." She turned and James heard her steps fade off.

"Mr. Rainwater." It seemed more statement than question.

"Yes, sir."

"Mr. James Allen Rainwater."

"Yes, sir." James felt his insides quake.

"I know who you are. You were one of the floor managers that day at Riverside."

"Yes sir." James hung his head.

"We wondered where you wandered off to. Looked all over for you."

"Yes sir." James felt his throat tighten.

"Where have you been all this time?"

"Everywhere." James shrugged. "No place in particular. Just . . . everywhere."

"I see. Why did you run, Mr. Rainwater?"

"I don't know. I didn't really intend to. It just sort of happened. I saw my buddy all mangled and dead and I couldn't stand there and look at him, so I went outside to get some air and I just sort of kept on going." James shrugged and looked up now at the sergeant. The officer was standing behind the sergeant, but he wasn't looking at James, but at his sergeant.

"So you never read about the case or anything?" Sergeant Wallace continued.

"No. I didn't need to read about it. I was there."

"Me too."

James looked up at him. Did he know him? Was he another manager?

"I got called out there that day. First time I saw something like that. I was just a rookie then. But I still remember seeing that. Mr. Johnson was pretty bashed up, all right." James bristled. Hadn't he just confessed to that? Why rub it in? "Blood everywhere. Legs all shattered. Concussion too, as I recall." James stared at the man. "Broken ribs, lungs pierced. Internal injuries." James was getting angry now. It made no sense for this man to torment him. "Damn near killed him." Why was he doing this to James? Suddenly James felt dizzy.

"What?"

"I said it damned near killed the man." Wallace looked at James and James thought he saw something like a smile.

"What?" James tried to make sense of what he had heard.

"Donald Johnson was critically injured that day, but he is very much alive and well today, Mr. Rainwater."

"What?" James had a flash of a memory of a road somewhere in the south, a flophouse in a port city, a church, a hot day, being hungry. "Wait. Donnie . . .?"

"Donald Johnson survived."

"But . . ."

"Yeah, he looked like a goner, I know. I thought he was too." The sergeant looked at his hands folded in front of him resting on the desk. "But he lived. Took a long time, but he got all better." The officer behind him bobbed his head in recognition and leaned over and spoke into the sergeant's ear and pointed at the computer screen. "Yeah, I got this, Klemper. Thanks." Klemper walked away as well. It was only Wallace and James now and they sat staring at each other for a moment. "I'm sorry you didn't know. Seems like a shame, you being on the run for something that didn't happen. Maybe if you'd stuck around. . . ." James still felt woozy. "In fact, your buddy got a big settlement from the company after that, as I recall. Paid his medical bills and some big amount for pain and suffering or something." Now Wallace fumbled with papers absently at the desk. "Something about a bad forklift that shouldn't have been there?" James dropped his eyes. "He's a wealthy man now, as I recall."

"Donnie's okay?" James looked past Sergeant Wallace, at nothing. "Donnie's okay."

"Well, I expect he can tell when it's gonna rain, and he probably has more steel in him than a tank, but yeah, he's fine."

"Then I . . ."

"You're not under arrest. There's no warrant out for you. Never was."

James started to stand, but this scenario was never in his thoughts. What should he do now? Where would he go? "So I can go?"

The sergeant raised his hand in a stop motion. "Your name did pop though."

"Huh?" James was frozen in a position half standing, half sitting.

"Your name did show up." Wallace motioned towards the computer screen. "Missing person's report."

James blinked, processing.

"Seems there's a Sarah Nelson who's been looking for you. Comes in every year around the holidays to see if we've found anything. We stopped looking a long time ago, of course. If man doesn't want to be found . . ."

"Sarah?" James sat now and stared at Sergeant Wallace.

"Yeah, your daughter?" Wallace raised his eyebrows. "Usually talks to me since I'm one of the few people still around knew about the whole thing."

"Sarah. You said Nelson?" James looked at the sergeant intently.

"Yeah. Sarah Nelson." Wallace paused. "So, you plan to go out and see her?"

James finally found a focus for his eyes. The sergeant's face was softer now, not scowling and not smiling, but somehow softer. "Yes, sir. I am. I do, I mean." James started to stand again, then he realized he had no idea where his daughter lived and no way of getting there. He looked back at Wallace.

"Maybe we should call first." The sergeant looked at him slowly. He picked up the phone, looked at the computer screen and called a number. When he looked up, he kept a gaze at James. "Ms Nelson? Ms Sarah Nelson? Yes, this is Sergeant Wallace, Cincinnati Police. Yes, Ma'am. Yes. Sergeant Henry Wallace. Yes, ma'am. We spoke last December. Yes, Ma'am." There was a long pause. Wallace kept staring at Rainwater. "Yes, ma'am. Seems we found your father." There was another pause. "No, he's fine. He's fine. He found us, really. Came walking in about half an hour ago. No, ma'am, he seems to be fine." There was another pause. "He wants to come see you. That okay? You sure?" James felt his stomach jump. "Yes ma'am. I understand. No, Ma'am. Yes. No, I can have a car bring him out." Suddenly James felt an almost overwhelming need to cry.

He caught his breath up short. Wallace looked at the computer screen again. "Yes, Ma'am. Still on Cooper? That's up in the Blue Ash area, right? Okay. It'll be twenty-five, thirty minutes. Yes, Ma'am. You're welcome. Yes, Ma'am. Yes ma'am. You're welcome." Wallace put the phone down and took a long look at James. "You ready?"

"Yes sir, I think so."

"I've seen these go bad, you know."

"Yes sir, I know."

"You came in here expecting to lose your freedom, I guess. You're free now to choose. You ready for whatever happens?"

"All depends on what you mean by freedom, I guess. Until just now, I wasn't free to see my daughter."

Wallace nodded assent. "Again, it's your choice."

"But I have to try, you know? And really, what do I have to lose?"

"Yeah, I know." He looked past him now and motioned with his hand. "Franklin. Come on over here. I got a job for you."

James Rainwater was loaded into the backseat of the cruiser, his packs next to him. They pulled onto the busy boulevard and he watched out the window at the city he had left so long ago. A few places were familiar, but much of it had changed. There were new tall buildings downtown. The ball park was different. The Village Pub where he and Donnie sometimes went for a beer after work was gone, replaced by a new sketchier-looking place. Some of the old neighborhoods that he remembered as being pretty rough when he had lived here now looked spruced up, houses repaired and painted. Then James let his focus blur and instead he saw some thirty years of his life, chaffered away on day labor and odd jobs in order to get through another day. And it was for nothing. He had met all those people, had been to all those towns, walked down all those roads. He felt an emptiness within him, a hollow void where once he had had something, even if it was only the conviction that he had to pay for his errors. But there was nothing now except a feeling of aimlessness. The route of the cruiser had changed from city streets to suburban lanes. Where would James go now? He had defined himself by his lifestyle. Maybe, in the end, his choices defined what he should do next. Perhaps he should ask the officer to stop the car and let him out. He didn't know what Sarah even looked like, what she did, whether she had children. She had married, evidently. Was she still married? He knew nothing of this life now. He had no right to come back. He had no right to come back and stir up the past. If he got out now, the officer could explain that he couldn't do it, that he was sorry. In the end, it's not like he hadn't disappointed Sarah and Sandy before. He didn't belong here. He would be doing them a favor, really. He needed to get back on the road.

He tapped in the metal screen between the seats. "Excuse me, Officer Franklin." She didn't answer, but pulled up along the side of the street next to a tidy split level house. "Officer Franklin?" James tapped again on the screen.

"We're here, Mr. Rainwater." Franklin looked over at the house and James followed her line of vision. It was a pretty little house, with maple trees in front, a basketball goal set up in the driveway, where a station wagon now pulled in and stopped. James was frozen. The door of the station wagon opened at the same time the door of the house opened. A blonde-headed woman stepped onto the front stoop of the house, staring at the police cruiser, then started walking towards James. The driver of the station wagon stood now. She was also blonde, but her hair was shorter. She walked towards a point halfway between the house and the police car. The two women glanced at each other, then back at James. James had not noticed that Franklin had exited the cruiser and now she opened his door. "Go on. I'll pull out your stuff."

James looked at his daughters who wore expressions of disbelief. They looked so much like his wife Carla did when he had left that he knew them immediately. The woman from the house would be Sarah, of course. She stepped closer then stopped some ten feet away from James. Sandy was behind her. They both stared at James with wide, watery eyes. What could James say after thirty years? "Um . . ." He lifted his arms slightly before him, as if to catch a hint of what he might be able to say.

Sarah took a step closer and cocked her head to one side just a bit. "Daddy?"

Afterword

Every road I've chosen has taken me where I am. I've always thought that if I didn't like where I found myself, then there was only me to blame. By the same token, I figured if I found myself with things going okay, well, just maybe I chose well somewhere along the line. I've always believed that, I guess. What it took me a long time to figure out is that just because I took a path that led me someplace I wished I wasn't, doesn't mean I had to live with it. Every day is a new fork in the road. Want to move on? Do it. Move on. Decide that moment to zig instead of zag. Of course, it wasn't always easy to break out of whatever rut I had fallen into, believe me, but in the end, it's as simple and as hard as that. Looking back, there are some routes I wish I had never traveled and others I wish I could choose differently, and still others I would do just the same. But they've all led me here, now, and now I get to choose again. Well, I have to choose, I guess; we all have to choose. But I look forward to it just the same. Maybe it's because, for a change, I like my options.

Credits

"Kentucky Backroad" originally appeared in *Mississippi Arts and Letters*, 2.1
"Dooms Chapel" originally appeared in *October Hill*, 1.2

About the Author

Author, artist and philosopher, Lawrence Weill writes articles and short fiction for both regional and national journals. He has three other books in print: *Out in Front, Incarnate,* and *I'm in the Room.* He also has poetry published in a number of journals. His artwork, including sculptures, paintings and drawings, hangs in several galleries.

Lawrence taught philosophy and ethics for many years at colleges in Kentucky and Georgia and his philosophy informs much of his writing. He holds degrees in mathematics, humanities and philosophy of higher education and has completed post-doctoral studies in both writing and philosophy. Lawrence has served in the roles of both academic dean and president at the college level.

An avid outdoorsman, Lawrence gardens, fishes, and saunters around in the woods of far western Kentucky where he lives with his wife Jennie in a house in the trees above a beaver pond. They also love to travel.

CPSIA information can be obtained
at www.ICGtesting.com
Printed in the USA
BVHW041358190622
640125BV00018B/167